12/15

Finder

Coal Mine Dog

Finder

Coal Mine Dog

Written by Alison Hart

Illustrated by Michael G. Montgomery

P E A C H T R E E
PUBLISHERS

Published by
PEACHTREE PUBLISHERS
1700 Chattahoochee Avenue
Atlanta, Georgia 30318-2112
www.peachtree-online.com

Cover illustration rendered in oil on canvas board; interior illustrations in pencil and watercolor. Title, byline, and chapter headings typeset in Hoefler & Frere-Jones's Whitney fonts by Tobias Frere-Jones; text typeset in Adobe's Garamond by Robert Slimbach.

Cover design by Nicola Simmonds Carmack
Book design by Melanie McMahon Ives

Printed in May 2015 in the United States of America by RR Donnelley & Sons in Harrisonburg, Virginia
10 9 8 7 6 5 4 3 2 1
First Edition

Library of Congress Cataloging-in-Publication Data

Hart, Alison, 1950-
  Finder, coal mine dog / Alison Hart ; illustrated by Michael Montgomery.
    pages cm. — (Dog chronicles ; #3)
  ISBN 978-1-56145-860-8
  Summary: In 1909, a nine-month-old gunshy puppy, trained unsuccessfully to be a hunting dog, finds a way to earn his keep when disaster strikes in the coal mine where his boy works.
  1. Dogs—Juvenile fiction. [1. Dogs—Fiction. 2. Coal mines and mining—Fiction. 3. Rescue dogs—Fiction.] I. Montgomery, Michael, 1952- illustrator. II. Title.
  PZ10.3.H247Fi 2015
  [Fic]—dc23
                                2015006673

To the many coal miners
who have sacrificed their lives

—A. H.

CONTENTS

Cherry Coal Mine

Side View

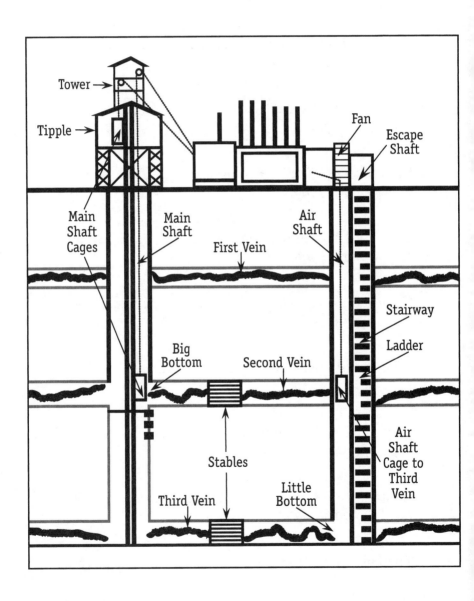

Cherry Coal Mine

Second Vein
Top View, Looking Down

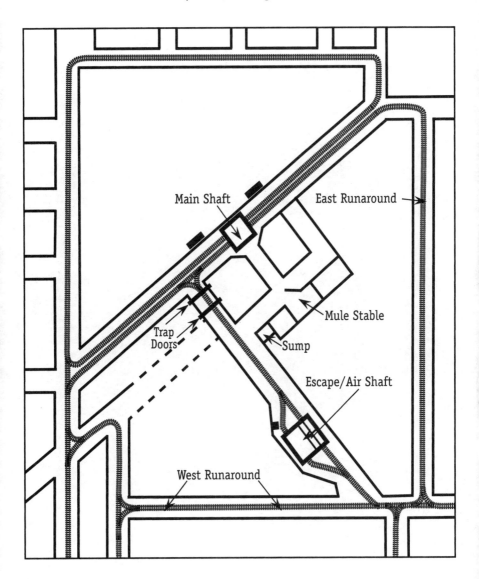

CHAPTER 1

Hunting

September 10, 1909

My nose twitches. I am on the scent of rabbit on the brush and quail in the tall grass. The rabbit trail winds into a mound of thorns. When I poke my head underneath the branches, the perfume of ripe blackberries makes me drool. I pluck a few from the ends with my teeth until the thorns prick my ears and I scuttle out.

Then I catch another smell. It's sharp and heavy, and I don't recognize the critter. The track zigzags into tall grass and I follow it.

"Finder's a straddler like Daisy was," a voice says behind me. "That means he works with his nose to the ground. Not like a drifter, who catches scent from the air. Straddlers are slower but the wind don't bother them. Our Daisy could scent a possum in a storm."

That's Uncle speaking. We're "training"—or at least that's what he calls it. Me, I'm just letting my nose lead me.

The pungent smell grows thicker as I come to a fallen tree. The trunk is rotten, the bark shredded as if animals have been scratching on it.

"What do you think Finder's hunting?" That voice belongs to my friend, Thomas.

We've both lived at Aunt and Uncle Eddy's house since early winter. Thomas arrived shortly after I left my littermates at Campbell's farm.

Uncle trains me.

Aunt scolds me.

Thomas loves me.

"Could be rabbit or possum. Or maybe the coon that keeps ripping down the corn stalks," Uncle tells him. "Let's hope the cur can do his job and keep his mind on the scent this time." Uncle's words are curt. I try hard, but too often I don't please him. "A hunting dog needs gumption. Daisy had it," he adds, his voice catching when he says her name.

"Finder's just a pup," Thomas says quickly. "He's still learning."

Uncle snorts. "By nine months Daisy was treeing varmints without a command," he says. "She didn't have to be trained—knew it instinctively. If Finder

3

don't start showing some of the same gumption, he'll have to go back to Campbell's."

"We can't send him back," Thomas says. "Finder belongs with us now."

"I know you love the dog, but we can't afford to keep an animal just for a pet like rich folk do." Uncle sighs. "Fact is, soon you won't have time for him. Summer and harvest are almost over."

"I'll always have time for Finder, even after school starts."

"Thomas…" Uncle hesitates and looks at the ground. "Your Aunt Helen and I have been talking. School might not start for you this year. I've already spoken to the supervisor at Cherry Coal Mine. You can start out digging."

When I hear Thomas's sharp intake of breath, I whine and lick his hand. All summer Thomas and I had fun in the fields and woods when we weren't training. We'd hoe the garden or pick coal from the slag pile. Then we'd splash in the stream and hunt for berries, mushrooms, and perfect sticks for Thomas to whittle and for me to chew. Those moments with Thomas made my tail wag, but now I sense that something is wrong.

"But my pa and ma didn't want me to work in the mine," Thomas says.

"I know they didn't." Uncle takes off his hat and scratches his head. I scratch too, at the flea nibbling my neck. "Except times are hard, Thomas. Farmers here in Illinois used to be able to live off the land. Now they can make more money *under* it. I'm lucky that they promoted me to mine examiner. Still, now that you've come to live with us, we've got another mouth to feed. We barely made it through the winter last year. You're fourteen, big enough to look eighteen, and Cherry Mine has good wages. You—and that dog—have to work and earn your keep."

"Sir, please don't make me quit school," Thomas says. "I'll chop wood for the neighbors and keep our stove filled with coal. Finder's strong—he can pull a full cart of wood or coal from the slag pile. And he'll get the hang of hunting, I just know it. We'll earn our keep. You'll see."

I whine again, hearing the unhappiness in his voice. I'd like to plant my paws on his chest and give him a kiss, but Uncle says, "The decision is done, Thomas." Setting his gaze on me, he commands, "Get your track, Finder."

Dropping my nose, I pick up that heavy smell again. It leads to the end of the rotten trunk, which is hollow and dark inside. When I hunker down, chattering greets me. I freeze. Two glittering eyes stare out, and I hear the click of teeth.

I like following a scent. I like working for Uncle. But I hate the sharp sound of the gun and the smell of blood when the critter falls dead. And it sounds as if this trapped animal aims to claw or bite me.

My body begins to quiver.

"What's Finder got cornered?" Thomas whispers.

"Sounds like a raccoon." Uncle says excitedly. "It'll fight, but it would've been no match for Daisy.

Let's see what Finder can do."

Slowly, I back away from the growling beast. The raccoon skitters forward and swipes my nose with sharp claws. Yelping, I leap up and bolt.

Uncle hollers, "Get back here and fight, dog!"

I run from the coon, crashing through the briars and tall grass. I don't want to kill it and I sure don't want it killing me.

I race down a row of drying corn stalks, the crinkly leaves whipping my stinging nose. Finally, I get to the other side of the field where the stream winds through the weeds, and plunge my bleeding muzzle into the cooling water. In the distance, I hear the crack of the gun. The noise rings in my ears, and I want to bury my head in the muddy bank.

Thomas calls me.

I want to go to him, but I can't. I want to have gumption like Daisy did. But even when my nose sends me in the right direction, my feet take me in the wrong one.

Thomas calls again.

Tail tucked, I slink to a hollow of dirt in the bank. It's cool and hidden. Curling into a ball, I wrap my tail around my sore nose. If I wait here all night, I can sneak home after Uncle is gone in the morning.

Aunt will be there with her broom. She'll shoo me from the porch and tell me I need a bath, but Thomas will hug me hard. He'll feed me bacon he saved from his morning meal, and for a while I'll forget that Uncle is right: I'll never be a good hunter like Daisy.

CHAPTER 2

Potatoes

September 11, 1909

There you are," Thomas says when I belly crawl toward the porch early the next morning. He jumps off the stoop and kneels in front of me. "You're a sight." He ruffles my neck and plucks at the burrs in my fur. He sighs. "I don't think hunting's the right job for you, but Uncle's determined. Come on, before Aunt sees you."

He whistles as he races to the shed. I follow happily, tracking the scent of bacon coming from his back pocket. The pigs squeal and carry on when we run past the pen. Sometimes I like to tease them, but today I'm intent on Thomas.

When we're hidden behind the shed, he pulls out a waxed piece of brown paper with a rasher inside. As soon as he finishes unwrapping it, I wolf down every scrap and lick the paper. Thomas pats me, but he's frowning. "Uncle shot the coon, skinned it, and put it in brine to soak. You'll be lucky if you get the tail." Brows furrowed, he checks my nose. "Coon got you good." He gives me a worried look. "Uncle says you've got one more chance to prove you're a hunting dog."

Staring up at Thomas, I wag my tail ever so slightly. I wish I could do a good job so Uncle would be pleased.

He jumps up. "Come on, boy. We need to prove to Aunt and Uncle that we can earn our keep. I don't want to work in the mine, and you aren't going back to Campbell's."

I follow Thomas into the shed. Sunlight filters through the slatted walls. He pulls out a feed sack and a pronged fork, which must mean we're digging potatoes. This time, he's also bringing along the harness and the wooden cart with rickety wheels. Thomas often hitches me to the cart when we bring coal home from the slag pile.

He pulls the cart to the potato field. I dash ahead, darting at the red-speckled chickens that peck in the dirt. They squawk and flap away, but the rooster flies at me with beady-eyed determination. Thomas laughs. "Leave them be, Finder." With a woof, I dash between two rows of brown-topped potato plants, my paws sinking into the soft dirt.

Thomas digs the fork into a hill and lifts up. He lets the dirt fall through the tines, leaving behind only the potatoes, which he carefully dumps into the cart.

"Ma and I used to do this every fall. 'Harvest on a warm, dry, cloudy day,' she'd tell me." Thomas's voice chokes up. I snatch up a loose potato and flop in the dirt to chew on it. "That one's green, Finder," he warns. "Give it to me and I'll toss it to the pigs. Ma says too many green ones can make you sick."

I don't know who Ma is, but Thomas's face grows

hot and red every time he says the name. For a while, he works in silence. I stay vigilant. The town of Cherry is not far away—the buildings are a jagged line on the horizon—and I can hear several dogs barking. I woof back, saying *stay away,* until their chorus dies down. Then I catch grasshoppers, crunching them between my teeth.

"Here, boy." Thomas holds out the harness. Panting, I stand quietly while he straps it around my back and chest. The harness hooks to short traces that attach to the cart. "What do you think, Finder?" he asks. "Would this be a better job for you than hunting?"

The little cart is piled high with potatoes, but I pull it easily to the shed. This is better than hunting, but not as much fun as chasing the chickens. Thomas follows with a sack of potatoes slung over one shoulder. He looks like a stooped old man. When we reach the shed, he spreads the potatoes on thick straw. "They need to dry before they go into the bins in the root cellar."

He throws the green and rotten ones to the pigs and then we hurry back to the garden. The empty cart jiggles and bumps over the freshly turned ground. Thomas unharnesses me and fills the cart again. When it's heaped high, he loads more potatoes into the sack. The sun is hot and I roll on my back, legs flailing in the air.

"*Buongiorno.*" A voice startles me. A young girl almost as tall as Thomas stands at the edge of the garden, holding a basket by her side. Her dark hair is covered with a shawl. Barking, I trot over to her. She pats me, unafraid of my noisy greeting.

I press against her skirt and slobber on her fingers, making her laugh. She smells of spices, bread, and the earth. I know the scent of this girl—not from walking Thomas to school, but from going to the company store in town. While Thomas is inside, I have to wait out front, tied to a post. I snarl at the town dogs to show them I'm not afraid, my hackles standing high. But the dark-haired girl always walks over, pats my head, and whispers, "*Silenzio, bel cane.*"

13

Thomas stops digging when he sees the girl. Sweat rolls from under his cap, and he wipes his forehead with his sleeve, leaving a streak of dirt.

"*Buongiorno,* Lucia," he replies. I run to Thomas's side, even though I would love to nuzzle the girl some more. For a moment, the two stare at each other. I bark, and Thomas tells me "quiet." Then the girl folds back the cloth on top of the basket. Bright red tomatoes peek out. I know what they are because sometimes when I'm very hungry, I sneak them from the small gardens behind the cottages in town.

The girl gestures toward the potatoes in the cart and says, "*Patata?*" as she holds out the basket and gingerly steps forward.

Thomas must understand because he nods and carries the half-full sack over to her. She sets the basket on the ground. I whine, wanting the girl to pat me again. She stoops and cradles my muzzle in her hands. "*Bel cane,*" she coos as she did before, the shawl falling to her shoulders. "Pretty dog."

Thomas hands her the sack.

"*Grazie,*" she says shyly. "Thank you." Leaving the tomatoes, she hurries off. I watch her as she heads down the dirt road for Cherry. Her skirts swish about her legs and her bare feet make puffs of dust rise in the air.

"Lucia's one of the immigrants who moved here when the mine opened," Thomas says. "Pa used to say the immigrants in Cherry had many stories to tell."

I lick his face. *Pa. Ma.* Thomas says both those words with sadness. I push my head under his arm. "Let's dig the last row of potatoes and then take the tomatoes to Aunt Helen," he says. "She'll be pleased."

We finish putting the potatoes in the shed. At the house Aunt is hanging wash on the line. Today Aunt smells like lavender soap and boiled cabbage. She wears long, billowy skirts, and I like to plow my nose underneath them until she swats me away with a damp towel.

Thomas shows her the basket of tomatoes. "One of the Italian girls traded them for half a sack of potatoes."

Aunt nods. "The Tonellis' tomatoes are especially firm and sweet. I'll throw several in with tonight's stew and then preserve the rest. Thank you, Thomas."

"Finder and I brought in two carts of potatoes as well," he adds. "That should help get us through the winter."

Aunt raises one brow. "Two cartloads will only get us through a month or two. Then we will need to trade with others or buy from the company store." She shakes out a wet shirt and hangs it on the line. As it snaps in the wind, a whistle shrieks from the tower rising to the northwest of town. Brick and stone buildings cluster around the tower. Behind it is the slag pile where Thomas and I pick coal.

"That's the 11:00 a.m. whistle," Aunt says. "Your uncle left for work before sunup and I'm guessing he'll be too busy to eat his lunch. Last night he found weakened timbers in one of the mine shafts and had the men replace it before the workers arrived this morning. He takes his responsibilities seriously." She turns to Thomas. "The safety of the men in the mine is his priority. *Your* safety would be his priority."

Thomas frowns. "Yes, ma'am. I understand. You and Uncle George have been good to me since my parents died. But, please, Aunt Helen, I don't want to work in the mine." He twirls his cap nervously. I nuzzle his hands, which smell of potatoes and dirt, but it's as if he doesn't know I am there. "Pa died alone in that tunnel. Don't send me below too."

She bends down and pulls another shirt from her basket. "It is already done, Thomas. You start tomorrow."

"*Nooooo!*" Thomas's howl startles me. "Pa was your brother! You know he wanted something better for me. You know he didn't want me to follow him into the mine."

Aunt's eyes snap like the shirts on the line. "Your father is the reason we are in this situation. When he died, he left your mother deep in debt. He owed the company store almost a thousand dollars. When she grew sick, there was no money to pay the doctor, and when she died, no money for the funeral. Your uncle had to take a loan out on this land." She sweeps her hand in the air. "Now we must pay off the debt or lose the farm. That means you need to do your part, Thomas. There is no other way."

Thomas stares at her, speechless. I woof, wanting him to notice me. His hand drops to the top of my head. "What about Finder?" His voice is almost a whisper. I wag my tail, finally hearing my name.

Aunt narrows her eyes at me, and I sink to the ground. Aunt often scolds and shoos me, but sometimes she slips me treats too. Only now her expression tells me I've been a bad dog. Did I track mud on the rug? Dig up her flowers? Tear the wash from the line?

"Daisy caught rabbits and flushed quail, helping to keep meat on the table," Aunt says. "Finder's still frightened by a gunshot. I'm sorry, Thomas, that both your ma and pa are gone. That's too many loved ones for such a young man to lose. But if Finder can't hunt, there's no room for him in this family. Now go give that dog a bath or he stays out all night again."

CHAPTER 3

A Hard Decision

September 11, 1909

Finder...*stream*," Thomas says as he stumbles away from Aunt. His voice is thick. Grabbing a bucket and chunk of soap from under the pump, he hurries into the field. I know *stream*, and I lope ahead of him.

"I am *not* working in the mine," he declares. I stop and wait for him to catch up. His cheeks are flushed.

"And Aunt and Uncle are *not* getting rid of you," Thomas adds as we continue down the path to the stream. I jump from a rocky ledge into the clear, cool water. It feels good on my paws and belly after pulling the potato cart in the hot sun.

Thomas rolls up his pants and wades in next to me. He dips the bucket into a pool. "We'll run away, you and me," he says as he pours the water over my back. "I'd rather live like a hobo than work in the mine. I saw a man hop on the Milwaukee train once when it stopped in Cherry. He had everything he owned in a feed sack."

I shake, my ears flapping.

"Hold still," Thomas orders and I duck my head. "Sorry," he says quickly. "It's just that everything is going to change, and I don't know how to fix it."

I hear footsteps. It's Uncle. "Talkin' to that cur again?"

Startled, Thomas straightens. "Uh…yes sir," he stammers. "I mean, Aunt Helen told me to give him a bath."

I wag my tail. Uncle has taken off his shirt and boots and rolled up his pant legs like Thomas. His face and hands are black with soot, but his chest is white. A towel is slung around his neck. Usually Aunt washes him in the big tub by the water pump. Today he steps into the shallows beside us, closes his eyes, and sighs.

As Thomas rinses me, he watches Uncle.

Eyes still closed, Uncle finally says, "We meet with Mr. Norberg tomorrow morning. He's assistant manager. A fair man. I've told him you are responsible and a hard worker. He's accepted my suggestion that you start as a digger."

Abruptly, Thomas lets go of my collar. I bound from the stream, happily shaking water everywhere.

Opening his eyes, Uncle takes the bucket from Thomas. "The company needs a wiry boy like you to work the narrow tunnels," he continues as he soaps his arms, face, and neck. "Mister Norberg agreed as a favor to me. Most young'uns start as breaker boys or trappers—thankless jobs with low wages. If you work hard, you should be able to pay off your Pa's debt in ten years or so."

Thomas doesn't say a word the whole time Uncle

is talking. I prance in front of him, feeling good since my bath. But he only stares at Uncle, who is dumping water over his own head.

"You can use your father's equipment—your aunt saved it in the trunk in the cellar. I'll wake you at five. First whistle blows at six." Uncle wipes his face and then dries himself with the towel. "I also think I've got a way to cure Finder from being gun-shy. If the dog's to stay on the farm, he has to earn his way too."

His tone sounds harsh and I duck my head.

Uncle hands Thomas the damp towel as he wades out of the stream. "Now hurry and dry yourself. Supper will soon be on the table."

Thomas watches him climb the bank and walk toward the house.

Grabbing a stick in my teeth, I leap into the water and thrust it into Thomas's hand. He takes it and furiously slings it all the way to the grassy slope beyond the ledge.

When I bring it back, he throws it again and again. Finally, he steps out of the shallow water and plods up the bank. Panting and exhausted, I lie down at his feet.

"*Ten years*," Thomas says, his voice tight. "Ten long years working to pay off the debt." He sinks onto the grass with a groan.

I crawl over and lay my head on his wet pant leg. His fingers stroke my ears, and I heave a sigh. I hate to see him unhappy. Jumping up, I lick his face. Only he doesn't smile, and when I pick up the stick and drop it in his lap, his gaze is far away.

∼

That night, I sprawl on the rug by Thomas's bed, dreaming of raccoons with sharp teeth. Then a toe nudges me. "Wake up, Finder. I can't sleep."

Thomas lights a lantern. I curl into a ball, tired from pulling the cart and fetching sticks, but Thomas nudges me again. "Come on. I need company in the cellar."

Yawning, I follow him from the room, toenails

clicking on the wood floor. The lantern light makes wavy shadows along the walls as we sneak past Aunt and Uncle's door, into the kitchen, and then outside. Cicadas and tree frogs chirp and a screech owl warbles. We hurry to the side of the house.

The cellar doors open from the outside to steep steps that disappear into the damp. Holding the lamp in front of him, Thomas leads the way.

The last time I was in the cellar was when Aunt locked me down there to hunt rats. Only the rats were smarter and faster than I was. Those sneaky critters scurried around boxes and barrels, which I toppled over when I tried to get at them. When Aunt let me out, I was draped with cobwebs and the cellar was a disaster. "Can't that dog do any job right?" she'd scolded.

Thomas hangs the lantern on a hook next to shelves filled with jars and crocks of food. A ham hock hangs in one corner, and I lick my lips at the salty smell.

"Uncle said Pa's mining equipment is in the trunk.

I haven't looked in it since I came to live here."

He moves to the other side of the shelves and kneels in front of the trunk. He opens the lid. Curious, I peer inside. There's a jumble of strange odors, but when he holds up a small blanket, I smell Thomas.

"Ma must've saved this from when I was a baby." He rummages through the trunk while I snuffle around for those rats. I hear scratching noises like tiny claws on wood, so I know they're scampering in the corners and on the shelves, taunting me.

Thomas calls me over. "Look, Finder." In his hand is a small black box. "This is Pa's old Brownie camera. He loved taking photos." Digging deeper, Thomas pulls out several pieces of slick paper. "Here are pictures of Ma that he took. See how beautiful she was?"

Thomas looks at the pictures. "Might be I could learn to use the camera like Pa. He wanted to be a photographer, not a miner." He loops the Brownie strap around his shoulder and then again reaches into the trunk, this time pulling out a hat.

It's made of canvas, like the one Uncle wears when he heads to work. A metal lamp pokes out from the front. It looks like one of Aunt's teapots, only smaller. Thomas also pulls out a sharp tool. "Pa was wearing this hat and holding this pickax when they found him under the avalanche of rock. See? The lamp is dented." He scowls and his lower lip begins to tremble. "Tomorrow I'll start at the mine like Pa did when we moved here. That means there won't be time to play fetch and wander the fields with you, Finder."

Thomas digs his fingers into the ruff of fur around my neck, and I nuzzle his cheek to let him know he's my friend no matter what.

"Ten years. By then the coal dust and damp will have ruined me with black lung—or worse." Thomas swipes his hands across his eyes and sets the cap on his head. He stands, the pickax still clutched in his hand. "Yet Uncle's right, Finder, I have to work. Helping to pay off Pa's debt is the honorable thing to do—even if it kills me."

CHAPTER 4

Missing Thomas

September 12, 1909

U ncle is sitting at the table when Thomas and I come into the kitchen the next morning. Thomas sets the pick and canvas hat he found in the cellar last night on an empty chair. Then he sits down and leans over to tie his hobnail boots. Silently, Aunt places a mug of coffee and plate of bacon and eggs in front of him. I sit beside his chair and lick my chops hopefully.

"Coffee?" Thomas asks her, sounding puzzled.

Uncle nods and dunks a biscuit into his cup. "If you're old enough for the mine, you're old enough for coffee."

A strand of drool hangs from my mouth as Thomas digs into his breakfast. Aunt sets a bowl of bread soaked in bacon grease on the floor for me. Excited, I twirl once and then scarf it down.

"I see you found your father's equipment," Uncle says.

"Yes sir."

"The cap fits?"

"Close enough."

"Before we leave, I'll show you how to fill your lamp with sunshine and fit it on your hat."

"Sunshine?"

"That's what miners call the paraffin in their lamps since it's the only light they see all day."

He pulls a piece of paper from his pocket. "I have a certificate from the mine inspector," Uncle tells Thomas. "It says you're eighteen. All you need to do is sign it."

I lick the last of the grease from the bottom of the bowl and then glance up as Aunt hands Thomas a pen. He hesitates for a moment, but then quickly signs.

Uncle refolds the paper and puts it in his pocket. "First day will be easy," he says, standing. "They'll show you around, introduce you to some of the workers."

Thomas finishes his breakfast and rises to his feet. His face is pale, but his expression determined. "I'm ready," he says.

Aunt hands them both lunch buckets. "I fixed your favorite," she tells Thomas. "Ham and corn bread."

"Thank you, Aunt Helen." Thomas takes the pail, which smells like the salty cellar, and starts out the door. I whirl to follow him.

"Stay," Uncle commands. "Tie the cur up if you need to, Mrs. Eddy."

"No. He goes with the boy," Aunt replies sharply, adding, "For today, Mr. Eddy."

Uncle stares at her for a second then nods. "All right. But just for today."

As we walk the lane toward Cherry, I race ahead and then circle back. The morning sun is rising, the day is cool, and this feels like an adventure. I've never been to work with Uncle. Usually he leaves early, before Thomas and I are out of bed.

"Wasn't so long ago there was nothing here," Uncle says. "No railroad, no houses, no stores. Cherry was cornfields and prairie before the St. Paul Coal Company bought it. Us farmers resented the mine and the foreigners who came to work in it, until we realized we could make twice the money underground. And we wouldn't have to worry about insects, frost, or drought wiping out our crops."

"I remember moving here," Thomas says. "I was excited to leave Chicago."

"Your father wasn't. He was a city boy. All he wanted to do was take snapshots with that box of his."

"I found his Brownie in the trunk. I'm going to learn to use it."

Uncle harrumphs. "You should have left it there—that's what I told your father. There's no time for dreaming when you have a family to feed—or debts to pay. Fortunately, your mother was practical. She convinced him to take the mine job."

Thomas bends down and picks something up. *A stick!* I wag my tail and race ahead, ready for the toss. I snatch it out of the air and bring it back to him.

Uncle shakes his head. "If Finder can retrieve a stick, he should be able to retrieve a shot bird and make himself useful."

"He will," Thomas says. "I'll work with him in the evenings while it's still light out."

When we get closer to Cherry, the town dogs start barking. Other men dressed like Uncle and Thomas stream from the houses that line the street.

Uncle nods to them, but he does not talk or walk with them. "You'll be working with many foreigners, Thomas. Most don't speak English," he says in a low voice. "Some of the men hate the 'Eye-talians' and

Slavs that now work the mine and live in Cherry. I find them hard workers."

The crowd of men grows larger, and strange words and smells swirl around me. The town dogs dart around the men's legs. I snarl at them, telling them to keep away from Thomas.

As we approach the buildings clustered beside the slag pile, the smoky air grows thicker and the clanging, grinding sounds grow harsher. Thomas's hand drops to the top of my head.

"You sometimes met your father here after work," Uncle says. "But I don't know how much he told you about the mine. That's the tower." Uncle points to the black structure that rises into the sky. I've seen it from the slag pile, but never this close up. I have to lift my head to see the top.

"Coal is hoisted from the ground through the center of it in one of two cages. It's dumped into the tipple, that long building jutting out from the tower."

"Nice doggie!" Small hands pat my head as three

boys surge past and clamber up the steps into the tower.

"Breaker boys," Uncle explains. "They sort rock from coal all day in the tipple. The rock then gets sent to the slag pile on a conveyor. The coal gets dumped in railroad cars below."

"I know about the breaker boys," Thomas says. "Last fall our teacher said it was a pity they had to quit school so young and go to work."

An enthusiastic voice greets Uncle. "Good morning, Mr. Eddy." A boy about a foot taller than Thomas shoulders his way through the group and hurries up to us. He shakes hands with Uncle and then says, "Hello, Thomas, I'm glad you're joining the company."

"Thanks, Alex," Thomas says.

I nose Alex, who used to throw sticks for me.

"You remember my older brother, Bobby Deans?" Alex jerks his thumb toward several men walking behind us. "He's a cager—well, an assistant cager—for his boss, Alex Rosenjack. Me, I started as a digger like my Uncle John and his brothers." He puffs out his chest. "Two days under my belt."

"So you're not going back to school either?" Thomas asks.

"Nope. Earnin' wages now. Might be we'll work together." With a wave, Alex leaves us and joins his brother.

Uncle steers Thomas to an orange clapboard building. I stay close by my friend's side. There are no town dogs here. No trees, bushes, or birds like we find when we wander the fields. What is Thomas going to do in this place that smells of soot?

"We're meeting Mr. Norberg in the company office," Uncle says. "He'll take you below. I've work to do." He gives Thomas a solemn look. "It'll be all right. You'll see."

Mr. Norberg has a swept-up mound of hair and a bristly moustache. He doesn't seem to mind that I tag along while he shows Thomas the boiler room and the engine room. At the emergency hospital, we meet a man called Dr. Howe.

"The St. Paul Mine here in Cherry is the most modern and safest in the country," Mr. Norberg boasts as we continue our tour. "And one of the first with electricity. You'll be proud to work here."

When he takes Thomas toward the tower, I follow, ducking at every bang and screech coming from above. Narrow metal stairs lead straight up. Thomas and I both hesitate, but Mr. Norberg smiles. "Don't worry, the tower is ninety-two feet of steel, engineered to last a hundred years."

Thomas starts to climb; I stay right on his heels. Midway up, Norberg stops at a small wooden structure. "Every day you'll get check tags here from Mr. Powers. Hang one on each coal car that you fill." He hands Thomas several small metal objects. "You are paid by the amount of coal in your car, so the number on the tag helps the company keep count. You'll be number 160."

As Thomas stares at the tags, his face turns white. I poke my muzzle into his side, sensing something is wrong. His fingers close around the tags before he shoves them into his jacket pocket.

"Don't worry," Mr. Norberg says. "Every new worker has first-day jitters."

A grinding noise makes me spin around. Two coal cars from the mine below rise up through the tower in a metal cage. They stop, and a gate in the side of the cage lifts.

"The cars full of coal come up in a cage," Mr. Norberg explains. "The same cage that carries the workers to the tunnels below."

After a man pushes the cars onto a track, a dozen miners waiting along the platform climb onto the floor of the cage. "Ready?" Mr. Norberg asks.

Thomas swallows hard. "May my dog come with me, sir?"

"Sorry. He might scare the mules."

"Okay. I understand." Stooping, Thomas cups

my head in his hand. *"Home,* Finder. I need to go to work."

I whine. I know what home means, but I don't understand why I can't come with Thomas and work too. Mr. Norberg steps into the cage. Thomas follows, joining the group huddled in the center. I try to follow but a boot knocks me away. "Git now, dog."

I clatter down the stairs, my eyes on Thomas as the cage begins to move. Settling his hat on his head, he juts his chin high, like he's trying to look brave.

But even from this far away, I sense his fear. I bark, telling him not to leave me, but suddenly the cage drops, and Thomas falls through the tower and disappears into the earth.

CHAPTER 5

The Same Day

September 12, 1909

I wait. The sun has grown hot and I flop beside the door of the company office. Mr. Norberg returns from the tower whistling, but Thomas is not with him. When I jump up, the man tells me to go home.

Slinking off, I hide behind a railway car under the tower. The tracks smell like tar and the iron rails burn my paws. I find shade under the car and sleep until a whistle blows. I look up.

Men begin streaming down the narrow stairs, all black from head to toe with coal dust. I race over, touching each one with my nose, trying to find

Thomas. Then I hear him call, "Finder!"

He clomps down the steps and falls to his knees. His arms wrap around me, and I lick his face, leaving a clean stripe. "Why didn't you go home?" he scolds, but then he grins. "I'm glad you didn't. It was lonely down there."

The men cluster in the shade of the buildings and dig into their lunch buckets, which smell like boiled eggs and sweet potatoes. Thomas finds a spot away from the others. I watch as he opens his bucket.

"What have we here?" He smacks his lips, teasing me. I slobber excitedly. "Aunt Helen packed a little extra today—she knew you would be here." Ripping off a chunk of ham, he tosses it to me.

"Howdy, Thomas." Alex Deans sits beside us and opens his lunch bucket. His brother Bobby sits down as well, grunts a hello, then concentrates on his lunch.

"Hi there, Finder," Alex says and pats my head with a coal-dusty hand. "Me, I like dogs. But lots of the miners are superstitious. Bobby told me one time a stray showed up at lunch, and that afternoon a mule kicked Samuel Spencer in the head. Sam died on the spot."

Thomas stops chewing. "What did the stray dog have to do with it?"

Alex shrugs. "Nothing. Like I said, miners are a superstitious lot."

"My pa died in the mine," Thomas says.

"I remember. Last summer, right?" Bobby asks with his mouth full. "The timbers gave way. Your pa was just walking in the tunnel when the roof caved in. Uncle John said it was bad luck."

Alex points a piece of cheese at his brother. "We're orphans too. Live with our sister and her family. Our folks didn't die in the mine, though." He pops the cheese in his mouth. "Cholera got 'em."

"Do you believe in bad luck and superstitions?" Thomas asks.

Bobby nods vigorously. "Always." The whistle blows, and the brothers close their lunch pails. "See you below."

Thomas scrambles to his feet. I bark, ready for us to go home. "No, Finder. I have to go back to work. You can't hang around the mine like a stray. I don't need any more bad luck. I've had enough of that already."

Fishing in his pocket, he pulls out one of the metal tags. "Mr. Powers assigned me the number 160. That was Pa's number too, and…well…*he died.*" Thomas points in the direction of home and yells, "So go home, Finder! *Go!*"

Head down, I trot off, casting glances over my shoulder until I see that Thomas is gone from the mine yard. When I reach the house, I lap water from the pan under the pump and then lie down in the grass where I can keep an eye on the lane. I can see the tower in the distance, rising into the sky.

Thomas's hard voice echoes in my ears. Many times he's told me to go home, especially when I followed him to school. Never has he talked to me so harshly.

Sighing, I rest my head on my outstretched front

legs. A fly buzzes around my ears but I don't snap at it. The air is warm and soothing, and finally I fall asleep.

～

"Finder!" Thomas's call wakes me. I scramble to my feet and greet him with enthusiastic licks. "What a sight for coal dusty eyes." Laughing, he pushes me away when my tongue tickles his neck.

"Come on." He drops his cap on the ground, lifts one foot, and unlaces his boot. "Let's wash in the stream. I want to stay outside in the sun." A shudder runs through him. "After lunch, I assisted Mr. McKinney in the third vein—five hundred feet below the surface. Not even a bat would go that deep, Finder. Mr. McKinney's been mining his whole life." Thomas shakes his head. "Not me. No sir. When the debt is paid off, I won't work underground any longer."

We run though the grass to the stream. Thomas doesn't take off his clothes like he usually does, but wades quickly into the shallow water. I see a frog and dive in after it. "Whoa!" Thomas cries as he loses his balance and falls in. Streaks of soot run down his face, making black swirls in the water. With a whoop, he lies back, his arms and legs sprawled. I splash and dig, glad to hear his laughter.

Someone on the bank clears his throat and I look up. Uncle stands there, a rifle held loosely in the

crook of his arm. "The mine must not have been too terrible," he says.

Thomas sits up, water dribbling down his forehead.

"Out of the stream, both of you. You earned your keep today, Thomas. Now it's the cur's turn."

I stop splashing. The solemn tone in Uncle's voice means "no nonsense." The gun in his hand means "time for training." Obediently, I climb from the stream and sit by his leg. "It's time Finder quits running off whenever I shoot," Uncle adds as Thomas sloshes from the water.

We head into the field. Thomas, wet and barefoot, takes careful steps while Uncle's stride is determined. I trot ahead, nose to the ground. I want to please Uncle and Thomas. I *want* to be a good hunter.

"You need to practice shooting as well," Uncle says to Thomas. "Perhaps the dog will take better to the gun if it's you pulling the trigger. If that doesn't work, I'll try a more effective cure."

"A cure?"

"Yeah. Tie him up, put his food bowl down, and shoot over his head. If he shies, the food bowl gets picked up. The dog only eats if he doesn't run from the sound."

Thomas stops walking and stares at Uncle. "What if he doesn't eat?"

"He will when he's hungry enough."

Thomas gives me a worried glance. "Isn't there another way?"

"There is—he goes back to Campbell's and they beat him every time he shies from the gun. Soon he fears a beating more than the shot." Uncle suddenly puts a finger to his lips. "*Shhh.* I see a rabbit." Crouching, he points and silently hands the rifle to Thomas.

I smell the rabbit first, then see it. It's hunkered in the dry grass, ears flat, blending in. I take off after it. The rabbit zigzags toward a stand of trees. Out of the corner of my eye, I see Thomas raise the gun. I hear the boom. The rabbit flies in the air and falls limp. I smell death.

I skid to a stop. The boom echoes in my ears, confusing me, and I forget that I am supposed to be training. I forget that I want to do a good job for Uncle and Thomas, and I race blindly in the other direction.

CHAPTER 6

A New Job

September 19, 1909

It's been a week since the last training. The rope has rubbed my neck raw. My belly rumbles. The sun beats down on the side of the shed. I'm hidden underneath the slatted floor in the dirt hole I've dug in my misery.

"No food until you stop shying from the gun," Uncle declares every morning. He brings my pan of food but he also brings the rifle. When I go to eat, he shoots into the air, and I dive into my hole and tremble.

It's not just the sharp noise and hollow belly that make me miserable. I miss Thomas. Every day he leaves in the morning. When he comes home, his legs drag. Sometimes he cries, burying his head in my fur. I clean the sores on his hands with my tongue. We don't amble in the field, dig potatoes, or play fetch anymore. So my heart aches along with my belly.

Today the sun is low in the sky when Thomas walks down the lane. His head hangs; his lunch bucket bangs against his leg. My tail wags at the sight of him. He doesn't look up as he stoops over the tub of water at the pump. I bark, reminding him I am here. But he turns his back on me, and his boots thump on the porch. I hear Aunt greet him, then a door slams. I wait, hopeful, but Thomas doesn't come out.

I crawl under the shed.

Later, Uncle calls me and I poke my head from my hole.

"Supper, Finder," he says heartily, but he's carrying the rifle. Crouching, he places the bowl where I can smell it. "Rabbit stew."

My nose tells me that it would taste delicious and I drool hungrily. Still, I back deeper into the hole away from Uncle and his gun, and I hear him sigh with frustration.

Then I hear the rustle of Aunt's skirts. "George Eddy! This is not working! Finder is as stubborn as you. Anyone else would have realized by now that he is not going to eat."

"Well, if this cur doesn't eat soon, I'll be taking him straight back to Campbell's."

"He's not going back to Campbell's, Mr. Eddy. You love Finder too, even if he is not the hunter Daisy was. I know the dog needs to earn his keep, and I think there may be another way. Thomas and I were discussing it before you came home." Aunt bends and peers into my hole. "Come on out, Finder. There will be no shooting tonight."

Aunt pushes the pan closer.

Scooting forward, I give her a toothy smile and she unties the rope. When it drops to the ground, I twirl joyfully, then lunge at the pan and eat the meaty stew in hungry gulps. After licking the pan clean, I run to the house where Thomas is sitting on the porch steps. I flop into his arms and he holds me close despite my wiggling.

Aunt joins us, standing at the bottom of the steps. "Hear Thomas out, Mr. Eddy," she says to Uncle. "He has an interesting proposition."

Thomas clears his throat. "Sir, I have thought about this since I've been working in the mine with Mr. McKinney. He sends me deep into the narrowest tunnels. Sometimes I have to belly crawl to reach the end. I usually find coal, but once I fill the sledge it is hard for me to push it down the tunnel to the coal car. It takes so much time I'll never fill enough cars to pay off my father's debt."

Uncle nods but his brows are furrowed.

"Here's my idea, Uncle. Finder is small enough to fit in a tunnel with me." Hearing Thomas say my name, I bump him with my muzzle. "He can pull a loaded cart. After I fill the sledge, he could haul it to the coal car. Mr. McKinney says he's worked a mine where they used goats. And in England they use ponies. Why not a dog then?"

Crossing his arms, Uncle raises one brow.

"I told Mr. McKinney about Finder. He said he'd speak to you and Mr. Norberg." Thomas pauses and looks at Uncle. "Together, Finder and I could haul more coal, earn better wages, and pay off Pa's debt sooner."

For a long moment, Uncle is silent. Finally, he uncrosses his arms. "I will think on this and then speak to Mr. McKinney and Mr. Norberg."

Thomas's face brightens. "Thank you, sir!"

"Now, Mrs. Eddy, perhaps we can eat our share of that stew that Finder so enjoyed." Holding out his hand, Uncle helps Aunt up the steps. "Wash up now, Thomas."

When the front door slams behind them, Thomas leans down and whispers, "Don't worry, Finder. Uncle just *has* to say yes." He heads over to the pump, still talking. "Mr. Norberg and Mr. McKinney will agree because it means money in their pockets. I know it won't be fun like rambling in the fields, but at least you'll have a job and we'll be together again."

I trot beside him, wagging my tail. My belly is full, and I am happy to be free of the rope, the shooting gun, and the hole under the shed. I am even happier when Thomas begins whistling as he washes his arms and hands.

It's a joyous sound I have sorely missed.

CHAPTER 7

Into the Mine

September 22, 1909

The steel cage rattles up through the hole in the tower and creaks to a stop. The gate lifts, and a man pushes two coal cars onto the tracks. Once the cage is empty, workers wearing canvas hats surge onto the platform. This time I am one of them. I am wearing my harness, so I know that I am going to work. I have no idea where this cage will take me or what my new job will be. Right now, all that matters is I am no longer tied to the shed and I am with Thomas.

Thomas lightly holds my collar. "It's all right,

Finder," he reassures me. "Just brace yourself."

Alex and Bobby Deans step into the cage and flank us. "Dog's in for a mighty big surprise," Alex says with a chuckle. "My first time down I almost peed myself."

Two bells ring and the cage suddenly drops. I lurch sideways and my stomach rises into my chest. Boot heels squash my toes. As we're dropping, another cage holding two coal cars rises, passing us on its climb to the top. I look up—the only light above me glows like a moon, then disappears.

Moments later the cage jerks to a halt, throwing me against Alex's leg. When the gate lifts, several miners push past. Some of them eye me suspiciously, then move on.

"This is the main entrance into the mine's second vein, Finder," Thomas explains. "The miners call it 'the big bottom.'"

A line of empty coal cars sits on one of two sets of narrow tracks running to and from the cage. I pant nervously. Lightbulbs jutting from the stone walls cast a golden glow, so I can see Alex, Bobby, and the other men walking down the tunnel in different directions. I am used to the dark of the night, but outdoors I can see shapes. Here in the mine, beyond the lights, the miners fade into blackness.

An older man with a grizzled face strides up to Thomas. "Make sure to introduce your dog to the mules. I don't want a fuss later when they meet. I'll join you at the sump and we'll head to the air shaft to take the cage to the third vein."

"Yes, Mr. McKinney. Come, Finder."

I stay by Thomas's side as we leave the big bottom and walk down a short passageway. My nose fills with a mixture of smells: sweat, oil, coal, and dirt. It is similar to the slag pile except for the added odors of hay and manure, and...*something else*. When we pass a car stacked high with hay bales, I hear a growl and scoot sideways. *What is it?* Two round eyes stare at me from under the car, and I recognize the animal: *cat*.

Thomas laughs. "That's Snow White. She keeps

the rats away from the mule feed. She used to be white but the coal's turned her fur gray."

I give Snow White a wide berth. Thomas stops in front of a long row of stalls. I see the broad rumps of mules—just like the ones I remember from Campbell's farm when I was a pup—their heads buried in the feed bins in front of them. A trough of running water stretches the length of the stable. Pausing, I stand on my hind feet for a quick drink. A few men are brushing the animals or harnessing them, but most of the stalls are empty.

"Mr. McKinney told me there are forty mules here; they stay underground until they're too old to work. They don't see the sun their whole lives." Thomas shakes his head. "That won't be us, Finder. I don't want to be shoveling coal my whole life."

A driver leads a mule past us. A bell around its neck rings with each step. We walk past the stable to the sump, a marshy area covered with wood planks. Mr. McKinney is waiting by a canvas curtain. "The pump room's in there," Thomas tells me.

We follow McKinney along a single coal car track that leads down a passage to the air shaft. The air is fresher here and I breathe deeply.

"Hello, pup," Bobby greets me. He's shoving a loaded coal car onto the track from a cage smaller than the one we rode from the tower. A boy is helping. "This 'ere is the other Alex. Thomas and Finder, meet Rosenjack," he says.

Rosenjack nods. In the dim light his face gleams with sweat, though the air is damp and chilly.

Once they've emptied the cage, we step onto the platform with a group of five men. High above me, I hear a loud *whirrrr.* I look up and cock my head to listen. "There's a giant fan atop us, Finder," Thomas tells me. "It pushes fresh air into the mine."

Two bells ring and the cage drops. This time I brace myself against Thomas's leg. The ride ends quickly as the cage jerks to a stop.

"This is the little bottom," Thomas says, his voice slightly hushed. "It's the entrance to the third vein, where we'll work all day."

It's darker in this tunnel except around the stable, which is smaller than the one on the second vein. Mr. McKinney checks some writing scrawled on a slate hanging on a wooden wall. "Weak timbers in the east tunnel," he reads. "Engineers are replacing them."

Thomas hangs one of his number tags on a peg alongside others. Before leaving the bottom, everyone lights the lamps on their hats. Mr. McKinney leads the way, holding a safety lantern high before him. When I glance behind me, I can see Bobby and Rosenjack pushing another loaded coal car onto the platform. Then we turn a corner and we lose sight of them.

We come to a large wooden door blocking the passageway. A boy sits perched on a rock ledge by the door. He is holding a string tied to a piece of cheese, I hear a squeak and then see that a rat is sitting up on its hind legs, nibbling at the cheese.

"Morning, Seth," says Mr. McKinney. He pulls a wrapped piece of toffee from his pocket and tosses it to the boy, whose eyes are on me. The candy bounces off the rock and falls to the ground.

Seth scrambles off his perch to pick it up. "A dog in the mine, sir?" he inquires as he unwraps the toffee. He pops the candy in his mouth and opens the heavy door.

"I see you have a pet rat to keep you company," Thomas says.

Seth grins. "That I do."

The door closes behind us. A long, dark passageway stretches ahead. The glow from the lantern flickers on the rock walls, and I startle at the rippling shadows.

We walk alongside tracks and past empty coal cars waiting to be filled. I step around fresh manure, so I know the mules travel this way as well.

Gradually, the miners stop off at their work stations until only Mr. McKinney and Thomas are still walking. My ears pick up clinking, banging, and grinding noises. Then I hear a faraway boom, softer than a gunshot. Still, I cringe.

"Don't worry, Finder," Thomas says. "It's not a gun. The miners use gunpowder to break up the tunnel walls. Then diggers like me have to shovel and pick through the blasted rock."

We finally stop. Mr. McKinney pushes aside a canvas curtain and motions Thomas through. "I'll check on you at the lunch whistle," he says, handing Thomas the lantern. A second lantern is hanging from the wall and he lights it with a match.

A coal car waits on the track outside the curtain. "Let's hope your dog will help you fill this today," Mr. McKinney adds before taking the second lantern and striding down the passageway.

"Mr. McKinney and I work in a 'room,'" Thomas says. "That's what the miners call them, but I don't know why. None of them has a bed or even a chair for comfort." He sighs, and I can see the sorrow in his eyes. I jump up, placing my paws gently on his chest, and he rubs my ears. "Before you came, I worked this room alone. Now I'll have someone to talk to and"—he lowers his voice to a hush—"I won't be so afraid. Uncle says I'll get used to the dark, but I doubt it. To me this place feels like the purgatory that Preacher Smith talks about on Sunday."

Thomas unhooks the rope attached to my collar, then picks up the lantern. I follow him as he parts the curtain. He leaves his lunch bucket by the entrance along with a canteen of water. Then we travel down a smaller passageway, which gets narrower until Thomas has to stoop. He stops by a wooden cart and sets down the lantern.

"This will be your cart, Finder. Uncle helped me screw axles and wheels to the sledge and add traces. You'll pull it to the coal car after I fill it."

Squeezing around the cart, Thomas pulls on gloves, then drops to his hands and knees. The weak flame on his hat dimly lights the end of the tunnel. I crawl along after him until the only thing in front of us is solid rock. I feel trapped, as if I'm down a groundhog hole with no escape.

"See this?" Sitting down with his back against one side, Thomas traces his finger along a seam of black, which glitters like gold in the beam from his sunshine lamp. "This is coal. This is what I have to dig out. It's what makes the St. Paul Mine so rich. And it's what will earn me enough money to pay off Pa's debt."

Using a chisel, hammer, and pick, Thomas begins to hack away at the rock. When larger chunks fall, he scoops them with a small shovel and tosses them into the cart. He does this over and over while I rest. Once the cart is full, he hitches me to it. I pull it over the uneven, gravelly floor until we reach the canvas curtain. Thomas holds it aside and I haul the cart through the passageway. He quickly shovels the coal and rock into the larger car, and we take the cart back to the end of the tunnel. We do this many times, until finally a whistle blows throughout the mine.

"Lunch." Sitting by the lantern in the entryway, Thomas takes off his gloves. Blood dots the blisters on his palms, and I lick them gently. "It's okay, Finder. The skin's getting tougher every day. Uncle says it might take months for calluses to form."

He opens his bucket, and hands me a piece of his
bread. First I lick off the bacon grease smeared on
top, then gulp down the rest. Mr. McKinney sticks
his head around the curtain. He nods as if satisfied
that Thomas is all right and then leaves.

"We're so far from the little bottom there's not
enough time to go topside to eat with the others,"
Thomas says. "Too bad. The sight of the sun would
sure be wonderful about now."

When he finishes his sandwich, he pours water

into the top of the bucket so I can drink. The water feels good on my tongue and throat, which are coated with dust from the chipped rock and coal. Then I lie down beside Thomas and rest my head on his leg. *Is this my new job?* I wonder. When I was hunting, I could at least feel the soft breezes on my fur and the crinkly grass under my paws.

"I know I must work," Thomas says, his fingers stroking my ears. "And I am earning wages. But shoveling day after day after…" He shakes his head.

"It feels like death to me. Still, having you with me makes this bearable," he adds, abruptly pushing to his feet. He puts on his gloves and heads back to the end of the tunnel.

Four more trips later, the coal car on the rails is heaped high. Thomas adds one last shovelful, which he calls "topping it." Then he suddenly lets out a whoop. It's the first joyous sound from him I've heard all afternoon.

"We did it! You and me, Finder! This is the first car I have ever filled myself." Unhitching me, he shoves the cart to the side. I hear the tinkling of bells and see two mules plodding toward us down the tunnel. They walk in between the rails, one mule in front of the other.

"*Buongiorno,* Dominick. For once it is good to see you and your team of stubborn *muleos!*" Thomas calls.

My heart beats faster as the mules grow closer. The lantern light reflects off their menacing eyes. I duck behind the curtain and peer cautiously around it.

Dominick walks behind the last mule, a coiled whip in one hand. "I see you have filled a cart on your own. You are lazy, so Finder must be working very hard," he jokes. "Where is he?"

"Hiding from your mules."

I woof, trying to show I am not frightened. As Dominick guides the mules to turn around and back up to the coal car, I keep my eyes on their powerful hooves.

Grinning, Thomas pulls a metal tag from his pocket. "Pa would be proud of me."

"Yes. Your father was a good man, but rarely did he work hard enough to top off a cart."

"This is your number, Pa," Thomas says solemnly as he holds up the tag marked 160. "This cart—and the many more that Finder and I will hopefully fill— is in honor of you and Ma."

Tears glitter in Thomas's eyes. I jump to his side as he hooks the metal tag to the front of the coal car. Dominick climbs onto the car and clucks to the mules. They strain, then begin to pull the car up the track. Thomas gathers his tools and lunch bucket, and we follow Dominick and the mules down the tunnel.

Two miners are topping off their own cart in the tunnel ahead. When they see us, they call rapidly to Dominick in words I have never heard. He talks just as quickly back to them in the same loud tone. The two men glare at us as we approach, their bushy brows furrowed under their caps. Suddenly one spits a wad of tobacco at my feet and gives me a nasty look. Then both men pick up their equipment and stride ahead.

Thomas catches up to Dominick. "What was that all about?"

"It is nothing."

"It must be *something*. Mr. Galletti spit at Finder."

"It's nothing," Dominick repeats. "Their lanterns kept going out and they needed to blame it on something other than the black damp. So they blame it on the dog."

"Alex warned me that some of the miners were superstitious."

"Superstitious, yes. But mostly afraid," Dominick explains. "Mining is like going into battle." Halting the mules, he gives Thomas a grave look. "Remember, you are not the only one who lost someone in the mine. Every time a miner steps into the cage and drops down that shaft, he worries that he or someone he knows will be the next one to die."

CHAPTER 8

Coal Mine Dog

October 10, 1909

I can see why Pa dreamed about being a photographer." Thomas is hunched over, shoveling rock into the cart. I'm hooked to it, ready to pull. This is my job now, deep below the surface of the earth, tethered to a cart in the darkness. It is cold, hot, noisy, silent, hard, and tedious.

I do it for Thomas.

"Dreaming of something different is all one can do in this godforsaken place," he adds, grunting with each toss.

We've been in this same room for too many days

to count. Mr. McKinney says it's a narrow but rich seam. He sets explosives, and then scuttles away like a bug while Thomas and I wait in the main tunnel. My ears have gotten used to the thick silence—there are no echoes in a mine—and then the far away muffled booms. By now, I don't mind even the nearby explosions so much. Unlike a gunshot, these booms cause nothing to fall dead.

This morning Mr. McKinney blasted the end of the tunnel again, leaving another hillock of coal and rubble for us to remove. I am harnessed to the cart, and I sit in the traces and doze. Thomas, however, talks on and on as he works.

"A newspaper Uncle George was reading had an article about two brothers named Wright. They have built a contraption that flies like a bird. Can you imagine, Finder? Soaring into the clouds?" He breathes out loudly, and I see the rise and fall of his shoulders. I flick my ears and whine. He stops shoveling to look at me.

"No, I can't imagine you flying either. And the

camera's fun, but I'm not sure I want to travel the country like Pa wanted to, taking photos of stern-faced families for pay. We need our own dream. Ouch!" Thomas drops his shovel and rubs the back of his head under his hat. "Dang rocks. Why do they jut so low?" Leaning back, he whacks angrily at the ceiling. Dirt and pebbles rain on his face and shoulders.

When he starts shoveling again, silently this time, he doesn't stop until the lunch whistle blows. Then he drops his shovel as if the handle is on fire.

"Hurry," he tells me as he crawls over to the cart. "Dominick is joining us today. He wants me to teach him to read." Thomas takes off my harness and creeps along with bent legs to the front of the dark little room. I am glad to be free of the leather straps. I shake off the dust and trot after him, the rock ceiling brushing the tips of my ears.

Dominick is sitting by the entryway, a lantern by his side. His lunch pail is open, and I smell the cheese-sprinkled, fried cornmeal he eats every day.

"Lucia packed a slice of polenta and parmesan

for you, Thomas. Though she snuck in a sausage for Finder." He tosses me a delicious chunk of spicy meat. "She likes your dog better than you," he teases.

Thomas blushes. The girl who traded us the tomatoes is Dominick's sister. Sometimes when we walk Dominick home after work, she waits on the porch. I run up the steps to greet her, sure to get a hug and kiss.

"I've brought *McGuffey's Second Reader,* which is the easiest book I have," Thomas tells him. "I also brought *Treasure Island,* which is the most exciting."

"Read from *Treasure Island* while we eat," Dominick says.

Thomas takes a bite of his sandwich and opens the book. "Is your sister's English as good as yours?"

"Better. Though Papa forbids her to speak it."

"Why?"

"Because he wants her to marry a good Italian boy and not some foreigner like you."

Thomas turns red. Then they both laugh, and I leave off my begging a moment to howl with them.

A boom ends their laughter. "Mr. McKinney is skipping lunch to blast," Thomas says. "He wants us to fill five cars today."

"Good luck." Dominick prods him with his boot. "Now read," he says. "Then teach. I want to make mule boss soon, so I need to learn to read and write instructions."

"You'll make a good mule boss. Me, I'm not staying in the mine like you and Alex," Thomas says as he throws me a bite of boiled egg.

"What will you do then? Be a farmer or a grocer?"

Thomas shrugs. "Anything other than shoveling coal all day. Right, Finder? There has to be something else we can do."

I woof, hoping for more egg.

"Your pa always talked about being a photographer. Tomorrow, bring your camera and take a picture of me with my mules. Now for this adventure story," he adds, "before the whistle blows again."

Thomas flips the book open and turns to the first page. Pulling the lantern closer, he begins, "'Part One—The Old Buccaneer.'"

I lie down by his side and rest my head under his leg. With a tired sigh, I listen to the hum of Thomas's words and dream of my own adventure in the warm sun.

CHAPTER 9

Bad Luck

October 11, 1909

The next morning Thomas carries his camera with him in a rucksack. He arrives early to take photos of the breaker boys, who argue about who will get to stand by me for the picture. They tussle with each other and then tug me right and left until Dominick scolds them. Quickly the boys line up in two rows. Their faces and hands are scrubbed clean, but as I stand in the middle of them, I can smell yesterday's dirt and soot.

Alex, Bobby, and Rosenjack beckon to Thomas. "Come on, take our picture!" Alex says as the three stand at the bottom of the tower steps, arms around each others' shoulders.

Later, when we reach the third vein, Dominick hurries to the stable while Thomas checks in. Backing his mules from the stalls, Dominick leads them toward the lights. Then he poses between them, hands lightly holding their bridles.

"Look at the camera, handsome Letty and Buster," Thomas says as he bends over the black box. The mules flick their long ears and Buster brays as if laughing.

"Thomas, what are you doing?" a sharp voice asks.

I whirl, expecting to see Mr. McKinney. But Uncle is standing behind us. He narrows his eyes at Thomas and then glances at Dominick, who hurries the mules back to their stalls.

"Give me the camera." Uncle holds out his hand. "I'll take it home when I leave for the day."

Often we meet Uncle leaving the mine as we are arriving. Sometimes we see him in the second vein passages when Thomas drops off his lunch. Usually he has a kind word for Thomas and a pat for me, but today he seems angry.

Thomas holds out the camera, and Uncle takes it without a word. Then he writes on the slate near the office door, boards the cage, and disappears up the shaft.

Thomas sighs. "No matter how hard I work, Uncle still thinks I will turn out to be a dreamer like Pa." Turning, he hangs his metal tag on the peg outside the office and picks up a safety lantern. Mr. Norberg waves Thomas over. "Mr. McKinney is ill today. You can work on your own, or buddy with John Donna and his son, Peter."

"I'll work on my own, sir. Mr. McKinney blasted yesterday in both rooms and left plenty of coal for me to shovel. Besides, I won't be alone. Finder will be with me."

"Stay safe, then."

Thomas lights a lantern. "I will be my own boss today, Finder. Perhaps we'll take a longer lunch and read a few more pages of *Treasure Island*. What do you think of that?"

Barking, I twirl after my tail and then dart at Snow White. She arches her back and growls. Since I've watched her kill full-grown rats, I scoot in the other direction.

We follow the other miners as they fan off down the main tunnel to work. John Donna and his son Peter, two workers from Scotland, join us. The two break into song, "So that is your new Sunday bonnet? Well, Sue, it's becoming to you…"

Thomas sings along, and I am glad to hear him joyful for once. When the group reaches the large wooden door, Seth jumps off his perch on the ledge and announces, "My pet rat can do a trick." He dangles a piece of cheese from a string, waiting. Suddenly a rat darts from a crack in the rock and grabs it. Seth jerks the string in the air and the rat hangs on, swaying to and fro. "He's an acrobat in the circus, see?"

"One of them buggers stole my apple pie yesterday," John Donna says. "Ran off with my fork too."

The miners all laugh, except for Mr. Galletti. "Mind you keep watch on that door instead of messing with those nasty rats," the older man tells Seth.

"Yes sir." Seth swings wide the heavy door. We pass through, stepping aside for a team of mules hauling a coal car that was filled yesterday.

I trot beside Thomas as he wishes a pair of miners a good day. It's empty and silent at our end of the tunnel, and I can hear the creak and groan of the earth as it settles. Thomas is ducking under the canvas curtain when we hear a shrill whistle from the direction of the little bottom.

"That's an emergency signal," Thomas says.

My hair prickles at the fear in his voice. Then I hear the pounding of feet and men shouting, "There's been an accident!"

Dropping his lunch pail and tools, Thomas hurries toward the air shaft, back the way we came. His boots crunch on the gravel while I lope alongside. He trips over a rail, but scrambles to his feet and keeps running. Sensing his fear, I trot faster. Other miners join us as we race toward the little bottom, the flames on their hats flickering.

When we reach the wooden trapdoor, it is open. I burst through ahead of the others. Charles Thorne, one of the mule drivers, is leaning over Seth, who lies on the tunnel floor. A team of mules stands hitched to a full cart on the tracks.

Charles explains what happened as the miners gather around. "We were driving past when he suddenly yelled 'don't run over my rat!' Then he pitched right into the car and knocked himself out."

Thomas stares at Seth's limp body. The boy's hat is off, and I see blood oozing from a gash on his head. I nose his neck and lick his cheek. When he groans, everyone breathes a sigh of relief.

Thomas volunteers to go for a stretcher and Peter Donna goes with him. I stay with Seth, lying close beside him to keep him warm. Mr. Galletti drapes his jacket over the boy, and for once he doesn't scowl at me.

Soon Thomas and Peter appear in the passageway carrying a canvas stretcher between them. Mr. Norberg is right behind, a lantern held high. "Is the boy all right?" he calls.

"A right nasty cut," Mr. Thorne replies.

"Let's get him topside to the hospital." Mr. Norberg slides his hands under Seth's shoulders and nods to Thomas, who grabs the boy's ankles. Together, they lift him onto the stretcher. "Thomas, you come with me," Mr. Norberg says. "The rest of you get back to work. I'll send Joe Leadache from the second vein to man the door."

Thomas doesn't hesitate. He picks up the other end of the stretcher.

"I told the boy to mind the door, not the rat," Mr. Galletti mutters as he makes the sign of the cross on his chest.

"He's only a lad," Mr. Donna says, "doing a man's job. Someone should tell his mum."

"I'll make sure someone fetches her," Mr. Norberg says. As he and Thomas carry Seth down the tunnel to the cage, I stay close by. Seth groans again. When his hand flops over the side of the stretcher, I give it a gentle lick.

Bobby and Rosenjack are waiting with the cage. "We'll take it from here," Mr. Norberg tells Thomas. "Thank you, lad."

"You'll let me know how he is, sir?" Thomas asks as he backs away from the cage.

"Someone will."

When the cage disappears, Thomas's shoulders droop. With my own head hanging, I follow him to our room. "That could have easily been me, Finder," Thomas says. "Seth is only a year younger than I am." As he harnesses me, I feel the weight of each strap. "Time to get to work, Finder."

All day we work hard, taking only a brief lunch and no break. Thomas doesn't quit even when the last whistle rings. By the time he tops the fourth coal car, my legs are shaking with weariness.

"Done," Thomas finally announces. His face is black except for his weary-looking eyes. "We filled four cars ourselves, Finder," he says, his voice thick with dust and fatigue. "Uncle and Mr. McKinney will be proud."

With a tired smile, he hangs his tag on the front of the coal car. Then he unhitches me and gathers his things.

The passageway is quiet. The others have all gone. Thomas turns off his lantern and leaves it on the wooden shelf by the office. I peek into the stable and see Dominick washing Letty. The mule's eyes are closed as the water streams down her face, rinsing away the dust.

Snow White darts from under the hay car and bats at my tail with her paw. When I jump, she glares at me but doesn't hiss. Ducking down, I give her a friendly bark.

Bobby waits at the little bottom to take the last of the workers up to the second vein. I greet him with a wag and he scratches behind my ears. He looks as weary as we do.

"How's Seth?" Thomas asks.

"The lad came to as we were carrying him to the hospital," he says. "He asked if his rat was all right." Bobby is reaching for the bell for the engineer to hoist the cage when suddenly the lights go out. The mine is plunged into utter darkness. I tilt back my head, but it is black above as well. For a second there is no sound except for the drip of water.

Thomas fumbles for a match and lights the lamp on his hat. The faint sunshine sputters. Bobby is staring at him, his mouth open. "What in tarnation happened?"

"The electric lights went out," Thomas says.

"Can someone bring me a lantern," Dominick calls, "before my mule steps on my foot?"

"Be right there," Thomas replies as he hurries off the cage, me on his heels. Behind us, Bobby mutters, "I fear the bad luck is just beginning."

Thomas grabs my collar, as if needing me to guide him to the stable—though it is no darker than the room where we work. "Let's hope Bobby is wrong, Finder," he whispers. I can hear the worry in his voice. Turning my head, I let out an encouraging whine.

The startled snorts of mules and the muffled voices of other miners fill the mine like ghosts. Thomas's fingers tremble, and as I lead him to Dominick, I wish there was more I could do to ease his fear.

CHAPTER 10

Payday

October 16, 1909

Uncle George." Thomas says as we stride down the lane, "as soon as the first telegraph comes through, hurry to the mine and let us know the scores of the World Series."

Uncle chuckles. I feel his high spirits, though he has been up all night checking the mine. "And who are you betting on to win it all?" he asks. "The Pirates or the Tigers?"

"The Tigers, of course."

"Okay. As soon as I get any word, I'll head to the mine. The bosses are as eager to know as the workers." Stopping, Uncle places his hand on Thomas's shoulder. "You've worked like a man these past weeks. I am proud of you."

Uncle veers off to the tavern, where talk of the World Series must be reaching fever pitch. For a week, the only talk in the mine has been about baseball.

When we near Dominick's house, Thomas calls out. His friend runs from his cottage, buttoning his jacket against the chilly fall air.

I race to the front porch to say hello to Lucia. Her dark hair cascades from under her scarf. She stoops to pat me, but her gaze is on Thomas. He glances her way, shyly smiles, and then shouts, "Stop being a pest, Finder!" Bounding off the porch, I leap from one boy to the other, snapping at their sleeves.

"Today's payday!" Dominick whoops. "And it's Saturday, which means a day off tomorrow. A double winner."

Thomas grins. "For me it'll be a triple winner when Detroit beats the Tigers."

"Oho. You mean a triple win for *me* when Honus Wagner outhits Ty Cobb!" He punches Thomas on the arm, who playfully returns the punch.

I run ahead. The breaker boys usually wait for me by the tower for a game of fetch before the morning whistle blows. But today they are playing baseball with a stick and a rolled-up sock, calling themselves the Pirates and Tigers.

"Hey, Thomas, take my picture!" the batter yells.

"Not today," Thomas yells back. "Uncle put the Brownie away on a kitchen shelf," he tells Dominick. "He says I can have it back when Pa's debt is paid."

Dominick shakes his head. "You'll be an old man by then."

Trotting up the stairs, I climb into the tower and wait by the cage. I know the routine. This is my life now—I am a coal miner like Thomas and the others, hurtling deep into the earth each day.

When the cage arrives, we all step in. It stops at the second vein, where the smell of burning kerosene is strong. Since the electricity went out, the passageways are lighted by kerosene torches that flicker and sizzle. Mr. McKinney is waiting by the sump. He seems more thin and hunched today, and his voice is raspy. "The air shaft cage is not working," he tells Thomas. "We'll have to use the ladder and stairs to the third vein. Do you think the dog can manage?"

Thomas scratches my neck under the collar. "Finder will follow, sir."

We pass the company office. "Mr. Bundy, has the new wiring arrived for the lights?" Mr. McKinney asks a man who is checking a notebook.

"Not yet. I expect it any day," Mr. Bundy replies.

Turning left, we walk past the mule stable to the trapdoor in the air shaft passageway. Thomas opens it, then lets the heavy door fall with a *thunk*. Mr. McKinney lights the lamp on his hat and climbs down first. Thomas goes next. When his head disappears, I lean over the hole and bark.

"Come on, Finder. It's like the ladder to the hayloft."

But it is not. This ladder descends into darkness,

and I can see no bottom. "There are stairs right below," Thomas calls. "So come now, boy."

I don't want Thomas to leave me so I start down headfirst, trying to keep my paws steady on the round rungs. The ladder is slanted, but steeper than the hayloft stairs. I slip on a damp rung, and Thomas catches hold of my collar. He guides me the rest of the way, until I jump to his feet. "Bravo," he cheers.

From there we take many narrow steps to the next platform and then another ladder to the bottom of the third vein, which is lit only by torches. The swirl of air from the giant fan on the surface makes the flames dance.

"Seth will be trapping again tomorrow," Mr. McKinney says as we pass through the door. "His mother said he fears coming back, but she needs his wages." He shakes his head. "If I had a son, I would insist he be a grocer."

"Or perhaps an explorer," Thomas says.

Mr. McKinney snorts. "Aye, even that."

The door shuts behind us. Pairs of miners are hacking busily at the rock walls. Here, close to the trapdoor and throughout much of the third vein, no explosives are used. Blasting is done only in the few rooms mined at the far end.

Mr. McKinney leaves us to our task, which is digging in the first room. I hear him coughing as he heads down the passageway to prepare for the next blast. The sound makes me sad and I nose Thomas's hand, but he doesn't notice. He's still feeling joyous from this morning and he whistles as he puts on my harness and gets ready to work.

"Payday today, Finder," he says. "Two weeks closer to paying off Pa's debt." He scoops a shovelful, lifts it, and dumps it into the cart. Pausing, he puffs out his chest. "Perhaps I am becoming a man as Uncle says. Next time I see Lucia on the porch, I'm going to talk to her." He touches the brim of his hat. "I'll say, *'buongiorno, bella signora'*—or should I say *bella ragazza?* I'd best ask Dominick before I embarrass myself."

Thomas keeps working and chattering until the lunch whistle blows. Mr. McKinney sits with us, trying to eat. His cough is deep. When he spits into his handkerchief, I see a black stain.

Lunch is over quickly, and Thomas gets back to scooping and shoveling. I'm dozing in the traces when I hear gleeful voices traveling down the tunnel. It sounds like Peter Donna and his father. Thomas drops his shovel and makes his way to the curtain. I pull the cart after him, though it is only half full. "Is Detroit winning?" Thomas asks.

"Pirates, four to nothing in the fourth inning." Peter grins.

Thomas's smile fades. "There's plenty of time for Detroit to catch up," he declares.

"I doubt it. But there is good news—the company is sounding the whistle early so we blokes can join the others at the tavern," Mr. Donna says as he and his son turn to leave. "Pay earlier too."

Thomas cheers. He shovels the last load into the coal car, which a mule team will later pull to the cage. His metal tag hangs from the front. "Six loads, Finder, and it's early. Let's find Mr. McKinney and head over to get our wages. Money in my pocket will make a pleasant jingle. Perhaps I'll spend some at the tavern on a Dr Pepper—and maybe we'll buy a bone for you at the butchers."

Carrying the lantern, Thomas heads deeper into the mine. I bound ahead, staying within the circle of light, until I come to Mr. McKinney's room. I nose aside the curtain and dash in to greet the older man. Sometimes he hides a faint smile when he sees me, so I know there is a soft spot in his heart.

The room is shadowy. Mr. McKinney is sitting on the tunnel floor, his back leaning against the rock wall. The flame on his sunshine lamp has gone out and his lantern is dim. I woof, but as soon as I get close, I know he will not return my greeting.

There is no blood, and his face looks peaceful, but just like the critters Uncle shoots, Mr. McKinney is dead.

CHAPTER 11

The Beginning

November 13, 1909

It's been weeks since Mr. McKinney died. He was buried that Sunday. On Monday Thomas was assigned a new buddy. Now he is digging with Mr. Dovin in the third vein.

Day after day Thomas fills the cart.

Day after day I pull it to the coal car.

Day after day Thomas shovels and dumps the rock into the car.

Sometimes we end the day so weary that we can barely drag ourselves home. The evenings are colder and the sky is dark by then, so we do not wade in the stream or hike through the fields. Thomas falls into bed after supper. I curl on the rug next to him and dream of blue skies. Uncle wakes us before sunrise and we trudge to the coal mine once again.

Just as Thomas picks up a big chunk of coal and drops it into my cart, a blast comes from the tunnel outside. The earth groans in response, and dirt rains on my head.

"Let's get out of here until the dust settles. Go now, Finder," he calls. That's my signal to pull the cart to the rails in the main tunnel.

When we reach the coal car, Mr. Dovin tells Thomas he is leaving early. "My blastin' is done for today. The missus needs help with the young'uns. Eight heads with lice." He scratches his scalp under his cap. "I may need a washin' meself. You and your dog finish fillin' this car, and perhaps you can quit early as well. Payday, you know."

When Mr. Dovin leaves, Thomas sighs and leans against the tunnel wall. "Payday!" he snorts. "By the time the company store takes out the money I owe for lamp fuel and socks, I'll barely have enough to pay down Pa's debt."

Sitting in the traces, I raise one paw to shake, a trick Dominick has taught me. It always cheers Thomas. Laughing, he pumps my front leg up and down, and then pats my dirty head. Even after a chilly bath in the stream, my tawny coat stays tinged with black.

"*Buongiorno!*" Dominick calls as he drives his mules toward us. "Is your car full?"

"Need one more load."

"I'll be back later then. "Gee!" Dominick gives the command to his mules. They turn around in the tunnel and head back along the rails.

Back at the end of the tunnel, Thomas begins shoveling the last of the coal into the car. I lift my nose. The faint smell of smoke drifts toward us. The mules' bells fade into the distance. Except for Thomas's labored breathing, it is silent.

Suddenly, a noise like wind blowing through the weeds whooshes toward me from the end of the tunnel. Shadowy shapes dart alongside the rails and I hear the click of tiny claws. *Rats.* They scurry around the wheels of the cart and run between my legs with no fear of me.

I sniff again; the smell of smoke is sharper. Thomas swears as the rats brush past him in their rush toward the little bottom.

Something is wrong.

I woof at Thomas. He feverishly tosses shovelfuls of coal into the car. Sweat rolls down his forehead.

Straining at my harness, I woof again.

"Quiet, now, Finder," he says. "If the car isn't topped, my wages will be docked."

I bark louder and strain against the traces. I will *not* be quiet. The rats know. *I know.* Somewhere in the maze of tunnels, there is a fire.

"What is wrong with you?" Thomas stops and glares at me. The beam from his helmet bounces against the wall. Then he sniffs the air too, as he notices the smoke. But he only shrugs. "Yes, there's a fire. With the torches burning day and night, there's always a fire down here."

No, no. My whine rises into a howl. *The rats were not afraid before.*

Urgent voices shout in the distance and Thomas peers down the tunnel. Dropping his shovel, he unhooks me from my traces and harness. "You may be right, Finder. We need to see what's going on."

Panting nervously, I lope down the passageway, circling back to Thomas. The other miners are still digging along the tunnel walls. "Is there a fire?" Thomas asks, stopping at each area. Most don't respond—some because they don't understand Thomas's words, others because they are hurrying to fill their last cars before going home.

Gripping Thomas's sleeve in my mouth, I tug him toward Seth's closed door. A gray cloud curls from under it. Thomas calls for Seth and when there is no answer, he pounds with his fist.

When Seth pushes the door wide, smoke rolls through the opening. The boy's eyes are wide.

"Where's the fire?" Thomas asks. Seth's mouth flaps but no words come out. Thomas takes Seth's arm and pulls him along with us until we reach the little bottom. Smoke is billowing down the air shaft from the second vein. There is no sign of the cage.

Thomas leans forward and hollers up the shaft. "Hello! What's happening up there?"

"A hay car's on fire!" Bobby calls down. "Rosenjack and I are pushing it onto the cage. We're sending it down the shaft. Stand back and when it reaches bottom, put out the fire with water from the sump."

Thomas places both hands on Seth's shoulders. "Run up the air shaft stairs and go home, Seth. Your mother needs you." He gives him a shove toward the ladder, and Seth darts off without protest.

Several men are already heading up the ladder. Andrew Lettsome stands at the bottom. He waves to Seth. "Follow me!"

Thomas hurries to join John Brown, Ole Freiburg, and William Smith, third vein workers who are hooking a canvas hose to the steam pump. "Stand back!" Brown hollers as he grasps the nozzle.

Minutes later, "Look out!" rings down the shaft

from above. We hear a roar and a fiery ball hurtles down the chute. It crashes into the marshy sump. The flames are so fierce, they singe my whiskers.

"Lord, the cage is on fire too!" Smith yells. Thomas and the three men turn the stream of water on the hay car. The hose bucks in Thomas's hands, but in minutes the fire is out.

Thomas sinks against the wall, panting. I nose his hand. But then Andrew Lettsome rushes down from the escape shaft stairs. "The timbers above in the second vein are on fire," he tells everyone.

"Did Seth get out?" Thomas asks.

Lettsome nods. "I sent him with George Richards and his father. But it's pandemonium up there. We have to warn the third vein workers to get out."

"I'll go east," Thomas volunteers. Grabbing a fresh safety lantern, he runs back to Seth's door. I bark after him. *Wrong way!* But I hear the panic in his voice when he hollers, "Abandon the mine!" I know he will not return to the ladder until the miners are warned.

On he runs, shouting. My heart is pounding as I catch up to him. Instinct tells me we should get topside—fast—but I will not leave Thomas.

As he runs down the tunnel, several of the miners stare at him, not understanding his warnings. In desperation, Thomas shoves them away from the wall and points to the smoke spiraling through the open doorway.

Peter Donna and his father barrel toward us.

"Go up the air shaft ladder!" Thomas screams,

"The cage is on fire!" Then he asks, "Are you the last in the east tunnel?"

"I believe so," Peter says.

I am glad when Thomas heads with the others back to the little bottom where the hay car lies smoldering. But instead of leaving the mine, he runs toward the mule stable. "Dominick!" he shouts.

"He was in the far west tunnel!" someone calls back.

Stopping, Thomas gasps for breath. "Finder. We can't leave Dominick. We must warn him."

Holding the safety lantern high, he calls again for Dominick. My ears prick. *Is that an answering cry?* I trot ahead past the stable, following the rails, hoping to scent his mules. But moments later, the lantern fizzles, and Thomas and I are plunged into darkness.

CHAPTER 12

Finding the Bottom

November 13, 1909

My senses sharpen in the dark, and I hear the snort of frightened mules. I can tell by the scent that it's Letty and Buster. Dominick must be close.

Hands trembling, Thomas lights the lantern again. We jog toward the stables, tripping over pipes and weaving around abandoned coal cars. "Dominick!" Thomas hollers, and this time the answering cry is nearer.

Finally we find him trying to calm his mules. Letty's eyes are white with fear and Buster has fallen to his knees.

"Hurry," Thomas tells his friend. "A fire is raging in the second vein."

"I will not leave my mules."

"Dominick, you must! The cage to the second vein caught on fire. There's no way to get them to the surface." Thomas tries to pry his friend's fingers from around Letty's bridle. Tears are streaming down Dominick's cheeks and he won't let go.

"If we don't escape now we'll all die," Thomas says, his own eyes glistening.

Letty rears, pulling Buster with him, and I jump out of the way. Their fear is making them panic. In this state they will soon crash into us.

Then Letty strikes out with a front hoof, forcing Dominick to let go. "At least help me unharness them," he sobs as he pats Buster. "I won't have them die in their traces."

Thomas swiftly unbuckles Letty. Wheeling, the mules trot off deep into the mine. I hope they will be all right. But it is time to get Thomas and Dominick to safety, and there is only one way out.

I whirl toward the air shaft stairs. I look back. Dominick wipes his eyes and stumbles after Thomas and me.

When we reach the sump, steam is rising from the burned coal car. There's no sign of Bobby, Rosenjack, or the cage. A stream of miners rushes toward the ladder. Ole Freiburg still holds the hose as if in a trance. Thomas stops beside him. "Is the cage running?"

"No. The engineer hoisted it free of the burning hay car. But it has been quiet for a while."

"We warned as many as we could in the third vein," Thomas adds. "Dominick and I are going up the stairs. Join us, sir, while there's time to escape."

Ole nods, but I sense his confusion. "Why did no one warn us earlier?" he says in a hushed voice.

Get a move on, I bark as smoke rolls down the air shaft, propelled by the surface fan. Above the frantic calls of the miners, I hear the signal bell ring seven times. Then there is a hush. The great fan above the shaft has stopped.

"The engineer must be trying to keep air from fueling the fire," Thomas says to Dominick. He has been silent since leaving his mules, and his eyes are dull.

Thomas squeezes his shoulder. "Don't think about your mules. Think instead of greeting your mother and father...and Lucia."

"*Si, amico mio,*" he answers quietly. Then he gestures toward the stable, which is shrouded in smoke. "If we can find the mule trough, we can douse ourselves. It might help our chances."

"Finder, *stream,*" Thomas says to me. My throat is parched, so I am only too eager. My nose immediately takes me to the hose that snakes to the raised trough, which is still filled with water. Thomas and Dominick soak their hats, faces, and jackets. When they are dripping wet, Thomas helps me into the water and splashes me all over. I lap desperately before jumping from the trough. Then I hear a faint meow.

Snow White! Crouching, I peer under the trough.

The cat is huddled against the damp wood, and I smell her singed fur. She stares at me without blinking.

I whine and Dominick bends to look. "What is it?" He stoops, grabs Snow White by the scruff, and hauls her out. "I could not save my mules, but I can save their cat." Instantly, she curls into a ball against his chest, and he buttons his damp jacket around her.

We hurry past the office and head toward the ladder. Several miners surge from the east tunnel, fear etched in their faces. They elbow past us and quickly disappear up the ladder.

Holding Snow White against his chest with one hand, Dominick hauls himself up with the other. "Pass Finder to me," he calls from the top rung.

Thomas gives me a boost, raising me as high as he can. Dominick leans down and together they push and pull me to the stairs above. Once I am safe, I bark for Thomas to hurry. Then the three of us dash up the stairs to the second ladder. This time I climb

up on my own. I follow Thomas and Dominick, fear propelling me through the open doorway to the second vein.

Men crowd the passageway, fighting to get out. Without the fan, there isn't enough air, and many of the miners are slumped unconscious against walls. On one side, the stable walls are burning. I can hear the scream of the mules. On the other side, the miners who pushed their way past us to get on the ladder first are lying on the tunnel floor, where a broken timber has crushed them.

A mule trots by us, his bell clanging. A support beam crackles above, and then crashes to the floor. I jump aside, trembling.

"Finder!" Thomas gestures from the escape shaft stairs that lead to the surface. "This way, boy."

Panting with relief, I race to him. Dominick is climbing ahead of us, and I dash after him with Thomas behind me. Nine bells ring from above and suddenly the boys stop. I hear a *whirrrr* as the fan starts again, drawing the flames on their lamps straight up. The fan is running in reverse. Slowly, the giant blades gain momentum, sucking the fire up the shaft until the wood timbers that line it begin to glow.

"By God, Dominick, we must go back!" Thomas yells. "Before the stairs catch on fire!" He climbs down as fast as possible. Whirling, I leap after him. Dominick cries out as the wood on the stairs begins to burn. "Jump!" Thomas hollers, and his friend falls, landing on top of us.

Four men shove their way around us, hoping to escape up the stairs. I recognize Ole Freiburg and Mr. Erickson, a timberman who often helps Uncle with repairs.

"It's no use. The stairs are turning to cinders!" Dominick calls to them as he sits up. His handsome black hair is singed and his left hand is red and blistered. Thomas rips the sleeve of his shirt. As he wraps the damp fabric around his friend's palm, Snow White peeps from under Dominick's jacket. I give her a lick to tell her to be brave.

I press against Thomas's leg, trying to keep my courage too.

"Which way then?" one of the men asks, alarm in his voice.

"There *is* no way out," another replies as he drops to his knees. "We've been left to die."

"There might be a way out," Thomas says. All eyes turn to him. "The main shaft cage at the big bottom may still be running."

"Only there's no safe route to get there." Erickson gestures right and left. "The passageways are choked with smoke. And the timbers are giving way."

Ole Freiburg begins to weep softly. "There are no lanterns to guide us, no signs or rescuers to point the way. We will burn to death before we make it."

Thomas sinks to the floor, defeated. I glance from man to man. Dominick's head is slumped against his chest. His bandaged hand strokes Snow White. "Mr. Erickson," Thomas whispers. "My uncle worked late last night. He was home when I left this morning. Did you see him come into the mine? Is he safe?"

Erickson exhales slowly. "I don't know, son."

A sob catches in Thomas's throat and I lay my head on his bent leg. Then the lamps sputter. The air is stifling. As the flames on the hats go out one by one, the small group is illuminated only by the glow of the fire. All I see in their faces is exhaustion and despair. All I smell is smoke.

And yet…I pick up another smell. Lifting my nose, I sniff deeply. My keen sense of smell picks up a hint of fresh air, and instantly I know the way to safety.

CHAPTER 13

This Way!

November 13, 1909

I paw at Thomas's pant leg. He barely raises his head. I spin around and dance down the passageway in the opposite direction of the escape stairs, then I dash back.

This way, this way, I tell him, my woofs insistent. He raises his head, blinks, and widens his bloodshot eyes. "Finder," he says, slowly getting to his feet. "*Finder* can lead us to safety."

"The dog?" Erickson aims a dazed look at me.

"The dog pulls a cart like a goat," Ole Freiburg says. "How can he lead us out?"

"Finder has a hunter's nose," Thomas says. "He can scent a raccoon trail in the dead of night. Why can't he scent good air and safety? He and I have traveled all these passageways to the main shaft cage. If anyone can find the way to the big bottom, he can." Grabbing Dominick's elbow, he hoists him to his feet. "Come on. We have to try."

The smoke is growing thicker and I bark urgently. The men look at me and then over my head to the tunnel beyond. The kerosene torches have long gone out and it is pitch black.

Erickson shakes his head. "That's the east run-around. It's the longest way to the main shaft cage. He'll be leading us to our deaths."

"I agree." One of the men stands, helping his friend up. "I won't put my life in the hands of a dog. Let's go, Harry." The two shuffle away from the shaft, disappearing into the haze.

Overhead, the *whirrrr* of the fan blades suddenly stops. An instant later an explosion high in the air shaft rocks the mine.

Ole Freiburg gasps. "Sounded like the fan house blew up."

"If it did, it means no fresh air is coming into the mine at all," Erickson says. "We've got to get out of here. The shortest route is past the sump and stable. There's no time to waste. Come with us," he says to Thomas and Dominick.

Only I sense the fire is the fiercest by the stable. Taking Thomas's sleeve between my teeth, I tug him in the other direction. *This way.*

"Finder wants us to go through the east run-around," Thomas says.

"God be with you then," Erickson says. Seizing Freiburg's arm, he plunges toward the mule stable.

"I trust Finder," Thomas tells Dominick, who's looking longingly after the two men. "You must decide for yourself."

Dominick nods. "Snow White and I trust him too."

Thomas points down the passageway. "Finder, lead the way. Dominick, put your hand on my shoulder. We'll use the rails and the tunnel walls as guides."

I trot off down the east tunnel, turning from time to time to send them an encouraging bark. "Keep barking, Finder! You are our beacon," Thomas calls.

I stop. The air is slightly clearer here. But then I scent *fear* and hear snorts of terror. Coal cars clang and hooves thump against rock. The hair on my back rises—there are terrified mules ahead. A mule can kill with one swift kick. How will we get through?

I stop, ears pricked, nostrils flared. The stench of sweat and dung is on the right side of the rails. Crouching, I belly crawl against the left-hand wall. Thomas follows. Dominick, still holding Snow White, scuttles after us.

Finally, we are clear of the mules. My nose bangs against a wooden door. It's one of the trapdoors between us and the big bottom. I scratch the wood, feeling heat on the other side. My ears flatten. *What if the tunnel on the other side is burning?*

Thomas hears my scratching and shoves the door open. A man stumbles through and stops before us. Thomas lights a match, which flares for an instant. There is a haunted look in the man's eyes. "Are we near the big bottom?" Thomas asks.

The man shakes his head. "You can go no farther, boys. We are going to die here." Pushing past us, he lunges down the tunnel in the direction we just came.

"No! Don't go that way! It's too dangerous!" Thomas hollers. But the man ignores him and disappears into the smoke.

"The poisonous fumes have addled his mind," Dominick says weakly. "Or perhaps he's right. We will die here."

Thomas lights another match and holds it up. Dominick blinks, his eyes dazed. "We'll make it," Thomas tells him. "Just keep your hand on my shoulder."

The flame on the match goes out, but it lasted long enough to show me the second trapdoor ahead. When I reach it, I again scratch on the wood, hoping Thomas will hear and not run into it.

"Good job, Finder." Thomas pushes it with his shoulder, but it doesn't budge. "Dominick, help me get the door open."

"I c-can't," his friend chokes out. "I can't...catch my breath. It's...like a...rock is crushing...my chest."

"Let me take Snow White."

"No. Use your strength to...get us out of here."

For a second, Thomas pats me as if reassuring himself that I am still here. I cannot see him and he cannot see me. But I sense that he is weakening too.

I whine. *We can't give up.*

Using both hands, palms flat, he shoves the door. Abruptly, he jumps back and cries with pain. "It's burning hot!" He quickly sticks his hands under his damp jacket.

"We've got to get through," he says, slamming his shoulder against the door again and again. With a crack, it crashes open and he falls through to the other side. I bump Dominick with my nose, and he drags himself through the opening.

"We made it to the big bottom," Thomas says, sitting up. "I hear voices. The cage must be ahead."

"Only...I can't...go any farther," Dominick pants.

"Yes, you can." Standing, Thomas grabs his friend under his shoulders and lifts him to his feet. I dart in the direction of the main shaft cage, trying to show them the way.

Suddenly, a man bumps into me. Then another and another, legs and boots rolling me over and over down the tunnel and away from Thomas.

Yelping, I finally escape to one side. I hear a faint meow and a flash of white runs past me. I struggle to my feet, my ribs aching, and stare into the black. Where are Thomas and Dominick?

I weave through the men surging toward the main shaft cage. Their cries and moans fill the air. Finally someone yells, "Over here!" Then several bells ring, and I hear the clank of the cage.

Frantically, I go from man to man, trying to find Thomas, but again someone boots me in the ribs. When I struggle to my feet, I bark, *Thomas! Thomas!* Only there is no answering call.

CHAPTER 14

Rescued

November 13, 1909

I must find Thomas! Working my way again to the side of the passageway, I tip my ears. Men mill about in confusion; several fall in a heap before me. I leap over them and rush back the way I came. Thomas and Dominick *must* be there.

This time I steer clear of the stumbling crowd. *Not Thomas, not Thomas, not Thomas,* vibrates through my brain as I sniff trouser legs and boots.

Thomas! I find him slumped against the wall, his hands held in front of him, and I smell seared flesh.

Dominick lies next to him, unconscious. Snow White is gone.

Wiggling with happiness, I wash Thomas's face with my tongue. It tastes of soot and tears. "Finder," he whispers. "I thought I'd lost you."

I bark. The smoke is getting thicker, the crackle of flames nearer. *Get up, get up!* I grasp his sleeve in my teeth and tug until it rips. *Get up, get up!*

He pushes himself to his feet without using his hands and sways unsteadily. "We can't leave Dominick," he whispers. With his last bit of strength, he drags his friend forward alongside the tunnel wall. *This way, this way!* I whine, leading him toward the hoisting cage. I can't see it, but the scent of fresh air curling from the shaft beckons.

"The cage is this way!" someone shouts above the moans and prayers of the men.

I turn back to Thomas. He's heard the shout too. But suffocating from lack of air, he collapses. Dominick is still in his arms. A miner trips over the two bodies, plummeting to the ground where he lies without moving.

I race toward the cage. Mr. Norberg, Alex and Bobby Deans, and Mr. Dovin are guiding men onto the cage. I bark frantically, and Mr. Dovin holds up a sputtering lantern. "It's Thomas's dog! The boy must be close."

I lead the way past trampling feet to Thomas and Dominick. Dovin pushes through the jostling crowd. "The cage is just ahead!" he shouts. "Keep going, men!"

When he reaches us, he calls out, "Need help here!" and Alex rushes over. He helps Thomas to his feet and the two carry Dominick to the cage and onto the platform.

"Don't leave without me!" a man suddenly screeches. As the panicked miner lunges to get on the platform, his knee slams into me, propelling me backward. I crack my head against the cage's support beam, pain envelops me, and all goes dark.

"Finder. *Finder!*

Thomas is calling me. Are we going for a hike? Fetching sticks? Digging for potatoes?

Water splashes my face. I sneeze and my eyes open. Thomas exhales loudly. "Thank God, Finder! I thought...I thought..." Setting down the tin cup, he rocks me in his arms. "So many dead," he moans. "I couldn't bear it if you were gone too."

I lick his face, telling him I'm all right. Except my head and ribs ache and my nose and paws sting.

For a second, confusion overtakes me. *Are we still in the mine?*

Thomas's arms tighten around me and I look around. There is blue sky above and I am breathing fresh air. But I can still smell smoke, I can still hear wailing. And I see flames shooting high.

I whimper anxiously, thinking I need to save Dominick...or someone. "We're safe, Finder," Thomas tells me, his voice raspy. "We got out of the

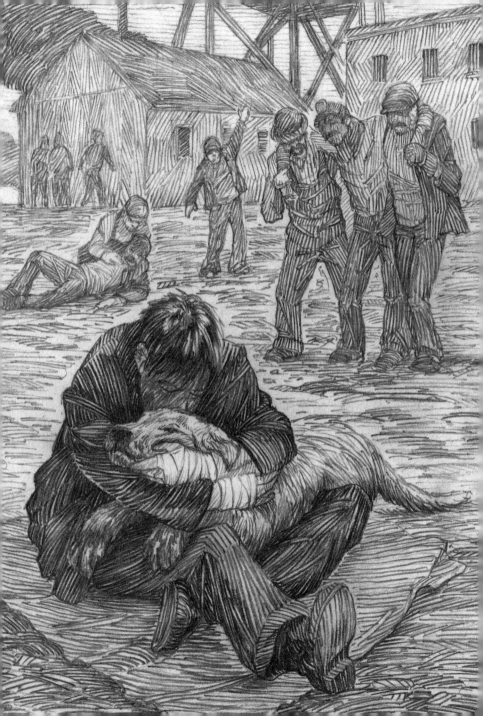

mine." Then I see we're sitting on a blanket outside the mine hospital. There are men all around us, some sitting up like Thomas. Others are stretched out, still. Men and women hover over them, applying medicine and bandages. Beside us, Alex Deans lies flat.

Dr. Howe hurries over with a leather bag. His clothes are ragged and smell of soot.

"Is Dominick all right?" Thomas asks.

The doctor frowns. "He's in the hospital. We're doing all we can."

"And Alex?" He nods toward his friend.

"Exhaustion. He'll come to when he's rested. How about you?" He checks Thomas's pulse and looks in his eyes. Then I notice the thick bandages swaddling Thomas's hands. "You came through better than most. Though it will take a while for these burns to heal."

The doctor strokes my head. "Hello, Finder. I hear you were quite the hero—as were you, Thomas. Peter Donna said you stayed in the third vein to warn the others. And despite your burns, you managed to get Dominick to the cage. Your uncle will be proud."

Thomas presses his lips together. "Uncle George…?" he finally asks.

Dr. Howe looks grave. "Your uncle's a hero too. He warned the miners in the second vein even though he didn't need to work today. But there's been no sign of him. Hundreds are unaccounted for."

Thomas stares at him, stunned. "Hundreds?" I wriggle in his lap, feeling the tension in his arms around me.

"The news is not good, Thomas. Are you sure you are strong enough to hear it? You are but a boy."

"I saw miners dying all around me down there, Doctor Howe. I am a boy no longer. Do not spare me," Thomas says.

"All right then." The doctor glances in the direction of the tower. "After you were brought up, the rescue party went down two more times. Nine more miners were saved. But during the last attempt, the rescue party was killed by the fire. The bell signals got mixed up and Cowley hoisted them up too late."

"Mr. Norberg? Mr. Dovin?"

"Thirteen of them." Mr. Howe clears his throat as if he can't go on. "I would have been one of them, except I was needed here."

"And the others—my uncle—are still trapped down there?"

"They sent the cage down unmanned in case anyone else made it to the big bottom. No one got on."

Tears fill Thomas's eyes. I nuzzle his neck. A crowd hovers near the entrance to the tower. I hear weeping. Even though I am too big, I curl into his lap and hide my head under his arm.

I hear a weak voice. "Howdy, friend." Alex blinks his bleary eyes. He's so black and dirty, he looks like a lump of coal. Scooting off Thomas's lap, I lick Alex's face and he chuckles.

"I'm glad to see *you* made it," Thomas says. "Most of Dr. Howe's news was bleak." He hesitates, then asks, "Your brother Bobby?"

Alex nods. "He and Alex Rosenjack made it out, but Alex is badly burned. And your uncle?"

Thomas shakes his head, then declares, "I can't sit by and do nothing." He stands up, his legs wobbly.

Dr. Howe grasps his elbow. "There is nothing you can do," he says. "Firefighters from Chicago and Ladd are sending streams of water down the main shaft. After that, the supervisors have ordered it sealed."

Thomas gasps. "That is sure death for anyone below!"

"They have no choice. The air being drawn down the open shaft is fueling the fire. Sealing it will suffocate the flames. Then a fresh rescue team with special equipment can get down there. Your uncle is a smart and brave man. Perhaps he will find a way to survive."

"But I have to do something to help," Thomas repeats. Alex sits up on his elbows to listen. I can tell by his drawn face and Thomas's unsteady stance that neither boy is ready to go back into the mine.

"You can do something. Go to your aunt, Thomas. And you, Alex, go to your sister. Her husband is missing below as well. Both have been helping the injured. And they are both frantic with worry." Dr. Howe gestures toward the hospital door. Aunt steps out onto the stoop, her face drawn and tired.

I bound over to her, ignoring my burnt paws. Her face lights up when she sees us coming to her, and she envelops both of us in her arms with a thankful cry.

CHAPTER 15

Back into the Mine

November 20, 1909

I am useless," Thomas says in disgust. He's sitting on the porch in a rocking chair, barefoot and bareheaded, staring at his bandaged hands. I am lying in a warm patch of morning sun. I can't get enough of the fresh air, the frosty grass, and the blue sky.

"Look, Finder." He thrusts his hands toward me. His fingers stick up from the bandages like bent claws. "I can't tie my boots or use a fork. Aunt has to button my britches, for heaven's sake." He sinks back in the rocking chair and gazes forlornly across the field.

Sitting up, I wag my tail. I am not forlorn. Every day I am happy that I no longer have to go into the mine and pull the cart.

The front door squeaks open and Aunt steps onto the porch. She is wearing a black dress. In one hand she holds a basket of bandages and ointment. The other hand is behind her. Does she have a treat for me?

"I don't know why you are going to the mine," Thomas says. "It's been seven days. Fires are still breaking out in the tunnels."

"I can help in the hospital," Aunt says. "And there is still hope."

I am hoping for a bone filled with marrow. Ever since Thomas and I escaped, Aunt has been generous with scraps. And no one has mentioned training or the rifle.

"How can you believe there's hope? All the rescuers bring up is more dead bod—" Thomas looks away.

Sadness fills Aunt's face. "It is more than one can bear, I know."

Jumping up, I bump my muzzle against her hand.

"But for your uncle's sake," she goes on, "I cannot give up."

Uncle. There has been no sign of him, and now his name is spoken with as much sadness as Ma's and Pa's.

Aunt gives Thomas a faint smile as she brings her hand from behind her back. It's not a bone for me—it's Thomas's camera.

"There are many stories to tell about this disaster," she says quietly, and after setting it on his lap, she hurries down the steps to the lane.

"Stories?" Thomas sighs when Aunt has moved away. "I don't want to tell stories about the fire or the missing. It's too sorrowful. Besides, how can I take a photo when I can't move my fingers?"

I poke my head under his arm. *Come on. Take a picture of me.* But he puts down the camera and pushes me away, then starts rocking the chair again, his thoughts distant.

Giving up, I trot off the porch. My burnt paws are still tender, and sometimes I cough up black gunk like Mr. McKinney used to do. But I don't want to think about the smoke and flames. I'd rather chase a chicken or roll in the dirt or...

"*Buongiorno, bel cane.*"

...or kiss Lucia!

I race down the lane and prance in front of her. She stoops and hugs me tightly and I feel her body shake as if she is crying. But she gives me a kiss, swipes at her eyes, and says, "I have come to thank you and Thomas."

Running back to the porch, I bark, *Look who's here! Look who's here!*

As Lucia walks up, Thomas pushes himself out of the rocker, holding his bandaged hands behind him. "I want to thank you, Thomas, for saving my brother," she says. "My family is in your debt."

"Dominick would have done the same for me. I only wish I had been able to rescue more men."

"As he wishes as well."

"Is he doing all right?"

"The doctor says his lungs may never be strong again. Dominick asks for you, and hopes you will visit him."

Flushing, Thomas looks down at his feet. "I haven't felt like—"

"I know," Lucia says softly. "The whole town is mourning. The Quartaroli, Armelani, and Cresto families have no word of their loved ones either. Please, come and visit. It would mean much to all of us."

Thomas nods. "I will."

She gives him a shy smile and then walks away. I trot after her, not wanting her to go, hoping she'll play. She stops to give me a pat on the head, then whispers, "Get him to come, Finder."

With a sigh, I watch as she hurries down the lane.

Thomas is back in the rocking chair, so I take the path to the stream to cool my paws and get a drink.

I'm standing in the water, lapping, when something rustles on the bank. I prick my ears as the rustling grows louder. *Rabbit.* Perhaps I can scare up some dinner.

Leaping from the water, I pounce, then hear a *hissss* as a paw bats my nose. Startled, I fall halfway down the bank. There's a cat in the brush arching its back. Snow White!

I charge back to the lane yapping, *Snow White! Snow White!*

Thomas jumps off the porch to see what the commotion is about. Again, I dart down to the stream. Snow White must recognize me, because she lets out a faint meow. I give her a lick. Her coat is brown and dirty, and I can feel her ribs under her matted hair.

"What is it, Finder?" Thomas asks as he strides down the path. The camera hangs from one strap on his shoulder.

Snow White! Snow White! I yelp.

He stops in his tracks. "Is that the cat from the mine? By golly, I thought she was dead." He slides down the bank and sloshes through the stream. Snow White flattens herself on the ground but doesn't run. He picks her up with his bandaged hands and gently holds her in his arms. "Amazing! Come, Finder. We must take her to Dominick."

When we reach the Tonelli's house, Lucia is sweeping the front porch. Her eyes light up when she sees us. "Dominick!" she calls into the house. "Mamma, Babbo!" She keeps the door open for Thomas, who returns her smile.

I bound in first, greeting Dominick's mother and father with loud woofs. Then I charge into a small room, where I find my friend sitting in bed under a thick quilt. His head is wrapped in gauze and his skin is raw on one cheek. When I jump onto the bed he begins to cough and laugh at the same time.

Dominick's mother charges in after me, flapping her hands. "Shoo, shoo!"

"No, Mamma," he says as he pulls me closer.

"This is the best visitor I could have wished for"—
His gaze lands on Thomas, who's standing sheepishly
in the doorway—"except for my friend, Thomas."

Dominick grins, and then starts coughing again.
Mamma fusses over him, speaking in a rush of
words, but he waves her away. "It is good to see you,
Thomas. What is in your arms?" he asks, raising one
brow.

Snow White pops up her head.

"That cannot be…?" Dominick's eyes grow wide.
Jumping off the bed, I bark at Snow White, who only
blinks.

Thomas nods. "It is. She looks almost as bad as
you," he jokes as he sets Snow White on the quilt.
"Her whiskers are singed and parts of her tail have
no hair."

Dominick strokes her matted fur, and she begins
to purr. Mamma and Lucia cluck and coo over the
cat.

"May I?" Thomas holds up his camera. "The
town newspaper could use a photo showing hope."

Mamma and Lucia huddle close to the injured pair. I put my paws on the bed, wanting to be in the picture too. Thomas fumbles with the camera and awkwardly presses the button. He tells everyone to stay in place while he turns a dial on the side of the box. "Let me try once more." I see him wince and grit his teeth, but finally we hear a click and he says, "Got it."

"Now Snow White must eat," Lucia says. "I will bring her a small bowl of milk. And a treat for you, Finder," she says, tapping me on the nose with one finger.

"I can't believe it." Dominick shakes his head when his sister and mother leave. "So many have died. The Chicago and Ladd firemen have put the flames out and cleared most of the tunnels. They've brought many bodies up—Ole Freiburg's body came up two days ago—but they cannot even identify most of them. For the cat to escape—it was a miracle."

"It was a miracle any of us escaped," Thomas says solemnly. "Alex and Bobby Deans made it, but the rest of their family did not."

"I heard the mine authorities spirited Bobby and Rosenjack out of town."

"Why?" Thomas asks

"Folks are saying they were responsible for the fire. That they didn't put it out quick enough."

"That's not true!" Thomas exclaims. "I saw how hard they tried. They thought they were doing the right thing by pushing the hay cart down the shaft to the third vein. Frieburg and the others put the fire out with the hose. But by then it was too late—the second vein timbers were already on fire."

There is moment of silence, then Dominick adds, "Yes, it was a miracle we escaped. A miracle—and Finder. He rescued us both."

Their gazes land on me, and I wag my tail. Thomas furrows his brow, as if thinking. He is quiet for a moment before he abruptly says, "I will visit again, Dominick. We'll finish *Treasure Island*. But there's something I must do now. Come, Finder."

There is urgency in Thomas's stride as he hurries from the Tonnelli's house and through town. When

I realize where he is heading, my heart plummets. We have not been back to the mine since the day we were rescued. I had hoped never to return.

Crowds are still clustered around the buildings, which are guarded by men in uniforms. We walk past the hospital to a white tent, where men are carrying stretchers covered by blankets. The smell of death is thick.

The tower still rises in the sky, but now parts of it are crumpled. Gas and smoke belch from beneath it. Men wearing helmets are stationed near the mouth of the air shaft.

Thomas heads for the hospital, where he finds Aunt tending to a man sitting in a chair. He pulls the camera off his shoulder and hands it to her. "Pa wanted to tell stories. But that was his dream. Me, I need to do something different. Will you keep the Brownie safe for me?"

"Of course."

"Finder and I have a job to do." Thomas heads toward the tower, slipping past a guard whose back is turned. I stay on his heels as he hurries up to a man holding a clipboard. "Who is in charge of the rescue?" he asks.

"That would probably be Mr. Williams from the Life Saving Station," the man replies, nodding toward two men wearing sooty coveralls and helmets. "He and Mr. Powell, the superintendent of Braceville Mine. But they're busy."

Thomas walks away, and I trot close by his side. Several bodies covered with canvas lie on the ground. Smoke and gas spew from the air shaft hole, and I shiver.

"Mr. Williams, I've come to help the rescuers," Thomas says. "My uncle is still below. My aunt believes there is still hope."

The man heaves an exhausted sigh. His face is as black as a miner's and his hands are cracked and red. "Son, there is naught you can do."

"We're forming another rescue party," Mr. Powell says. "But it's no job for a boy with wounded hands."

Thomas stares at his bandages. "I know I can't

shovel debris. But my dog and I can help with the search." He places his hand on my head. "Finder is used to the tunnels in the mine. He knows how to follow a scent. He rescued my friend Dominick and me, and he would have saved more men if the miners had trusted him." Looking up, Thomas squares his shoulders with determination. "So gentlemen, if there are any survivors trapped down there, my dog will find them."

CHAPTER 16

Uncle George

November 20, 1909

Mr. Powell and Mr. Williams glance down at me. I prick my ears and wag my tail, but Mr. Powell frowns. "A rescue dog in a mine? Never heard of such a thing."

"But, sir, isn't it worth a try?"

Mr. Powell shakes his head. "It's too dangerous."

Mr. Williams pulls Mr. Powell to one side. They talk in low voices, looking over at us from time to time. After a while, they return to where we are standing. "All right, young man," Mr. Powell says. "Mr. Williams here says you are George Eddy's nephew.

He told me of you and your dog's bravery after the fire. The rescue party will be ready to go below soon. If you believe Finder will be of use, then you can both go with them."

Mr. Williams puts his hand on Thomas's shoulder. "We are grateful for your offer, Thomas. We are desperate for help—and hope."

"Thank you, sirs," Thomas says. "Finder will prove that he is worthy."

"You know the risks?" Mr. Williams asks. "This is no adventure."

"Yes sir. My Pa died in the tunnels and many of my friends died in this fire."

"All right then." Mr. Powell gestures over his shoulder. "You'll need a special safety helmet and lantern."

Kneeling, Thomas holds my muzzle in his hands. "We're going below again, Finder." His voice quivers. "There'll be fires, poisonous gas, and falling timbers." As he clips a rope to my collar, I see that his wounds have bled through the bandages. "But this time, we aren't shoveling coal or pulling a cart. This time we're rescuing men."

My senses grow alert at the tone of his words. I circle, tugging on the rope.

Mr. Powell comes over and hands Thomas a helmet equipped with a lamp. "Are you and your dog ready?"

Thomas puts on the helmet and takes a deep breath. "Yes sir," he declares. I hear strength and determination in those two words.

I pant with eagerness as we stride toward the air shaft. I understand that I am going back into the hated mine. A week ago, I barely made it out. But my life was saved—perhaps now Thomas and I can save others.

"You must trust Finder to lead us," Thomas tells Mr. Powell when we stop beside the smoky opening, "even if it feels as if he is going in the wrong direction. His sense of smell and hearing are superior to ours."

Standing on my hind legs, I place my paws on

Thomas's chest. I know he is talking about me, and I hope I can live up to his words.

"It's up to you, boy," he whispers as I lick his face. "Get your track, Finder. *Find Uncle George*."

I drop to the ground and pull Thomas to the cage. The others in the rescue party—Mr. Castelli, Father Haney of Saint Mary's Church, and Captain Kenney—join us for the ride down on a makeshift platform to the second vein. The stench of burning wood and earth grows stronger as we disappear into the ground.

The only light is our lantern.

The cage bumps against the sides and halts at the bottom. There is more light here, but it is still hard to see. Several men are hosing down a fire in one tunnel. Others are shoveling their way through a cave-in. The air is rotten with scorched flesh. My eagerness vanishes. How will I find the living in this horror?

Then Thomas again commands, "Get your track, Finder. *Find Uncle George*."

Leaping from the platform, I follow the faint scent of fresh air. Thomas gestures for the rescue party to follow.

"We tried that way yesterday," Castelli says.

"The tunnel was barred by decaying mules and overturned coal cars," Father Haney adds. "We couldn't get through."

I lift my head and draw in a deep breath, trying to sense anything different in the smoky air. "The boy said to trust the dog," Powell replies. "Light your hats and let's try again."

I sniff along the corridor, tugging on the leash. The four men are close behind us. We step over smoldering timbers and puddles of water until we reach the south entry. Ahead are bloated mule carcasses. The men hold handkerchiefs to their noses and struggle forward.

The many smells confuse my nose, so I prick my ears to listen. *Are those voices?* Straining at the rope, I pull Thomas toward the faint sounds.

"He's got something," Thomas says excitedly.

There is a rustling noise, and a few rats skitter past.

"Only rats," Captain Kenney declares.

"If rats can live, then so can a person," Castelli exclaims. "Let's push aside some of these coal cars to make a path."

It takes a long time, but finally we are on the move again. When we come to a side tunnel, Mr. Powell calls for everyone to stop.

As the men discuss which direction to take, I prick my ears and stare into the darkness.

Because I *do* hear something more than rats. *Is it the shuffle of weary feet?* I pull Thomas a little farther into the side tunnel. That is when I smell the sweat of a living man. Lunging forward, I pull the rope from Thomas's grasp. *Over here! Over here!* The rescue team follows my barks as I weave around debris.

Suddenly, a person stumbles toward us from the dark, then another and another until there is a group of them. Stunned, they stare at us, squinting in the glare of our headlamps.

Then Mr. Castelli cries out, "Quartaroli!" The rescuers rush forward and the survivors fall into their arms. I twirl joyfully. "Praise the Lord!" Father Haney shouts and begins praying.

"Is it Sunday or Monday?" a survivor asks.

"We thought no one would find us," another of the soot-covered men chokes out between cracked lips.

"It is Saturday," Captain Kenney says. "You have been underground for seven days."

"Seven days?" another exclaims. "We lost track of time."

Castelli holds the first miner he had recognized and sobs, "I can't believe it is you, Antenore Quartaroli."

As the men hug and talk, I touch each of them with my nose, then turn to Thomas. I do not find Uncle George.

"Are there others still alive?" Thomas asks.

"In nine north," one replies. "George Eddy, Thomas White, Walter Waite, and others. Most are too weak to walk."

"Uncle George is alive!" Thomas gasps.

"I hope so. Some of them were injured and couldn't leave the tunnel. Be careful, though. It is a treacherous maze to get back there."

"The dog will find them," Mr. Powell says. "Castelli, make sure these men get to the surface and receive immediate care. Send more help as well. The rest of us will press on. Thomas, you and your dog lead the way."

This time I don't need a command. I know the name Uncle. My excitement rises with the hope in the men's voices. If there are more survivors, I will find them.

Leaping forward, I again yank the rope from Thomas's grasp. It flaps behind me as I dodge the charred ruins of the mine, my nose tracking the scent of the living into a low corridor. Abruptly I'm stopped by suffocating black damp. My head feels as if it is being crushed, but I shake it and force myself to go on.

In the faint light of the lanterns bobbing behind

me, my eyes make out a wall of rock. Several men are lying in front of it. One cries out fearfully at the sight of me, as if I am a ghost.

I woof, letting him know I am real.

"Thank the Lord! We have been found!" the man calls as the rescuers' lights come closer. There is a hole in the rocks behind the survivors. I stick my nose through and sniff. *Uncle!* Furiously, I start to dig.

Thomas rushes up beside me and shouts into the hole. "Is anyone alive in there?"

"Yes," a faint voice answers. "We are alive...and thirsty."

"Hang on." Before the rescuers can begin hacking at the hole to make it bigger, I squirm through. Uncle is lying on his side. His eyes are closed against the light beaming through the hole. I crawl to him and lay my head beside his.

"Finder," he croaks. His tongue is swollen but I know he is saying my name. His hand moves ever so slightly, trying to reach for me, and I nudge my nose under it.

When the hole is wide enough, Thomas crawls through, followed by Mr. Powell and Father Haney. Tears flow down Thomas's cheeks. "Uncle George. You're alive."

"Thank goodness you found us," Uncle whispers. "We wouldn't have made it much longer."

After the rescuers dig out a larger opening, they place Uncle and the others on stretchers and carry them one by one back to the bottom of the air shaft. Castelli has brought Dr. Howe into the mine, and he is checking each survivor.

"It's a miracle that you and these other nineteen men survived—for a whole week," Dr. Howe says as he checks Uncle's pulse. I lie down beside his stretcher. Thomas sits beside it, giving Uncle sips of water from a tin cup.

"How did you manage?" Thomas asks.

"Everyone took care of each other," Uncle says weakly. "We found a little water that trickled through a hole. I was so worried about you, Thomas. I am glad to see that you and Finder made it out."

"Yes. Dominick and I were two of the last ones rescued from the third vein. Thanks to Finder."

Uncle strokes my head.

"Let's get you to the surface," Dr. Howe says to him. "A team of doctors and nurses is waiting."

"And a bowl of rabbit stew?" Uncle asks.

"Perhaps in a few days."

Uncle sits up. "I will walk out of this mine on my own two feet," he declares shakily. He stands with Thomas's help and climbs onto the platform.

"It is night now, but the moon is out," Dr. Howe cautions. "Even that weak light may be too much for your eyes after so many days in the dark."

Uncle holds onto Thomas for support as the platform rises. When we break the surface, people press against the barricade around the air shaft, cheering. Two lines of guards have made a pathway to the railroad hospital car. Applause breaks out when the crowd sees us, but the guards quickly hush the people as if the noise will startle the survivors.

I search for Aunt in the sea of anxious faces. The moment she catches sight of us, she breaks into tears.

She runs toward us. "Oh, George," she sobs. "Is it really you?"

When Uncle sees her, he collapses. Thomas and Aunt flank him. Gently lifting him to his feet, they help him down the path to the hospital car where men in rubber coats are waiting.

I trot behind the three, slowing as the rush of excitement turns to exhaustion. My burnt paws are raw from digging. My tongue hangs from my parched mouth. The lights hurt my eyes.

A nurse comes up to guide Aunt and Uncle into the hospital car. Thomas stops at the steps to make sure they get into the car safely. Then he turns to search for me.

Dropping to his knees, he hauls me into his arms. "You did it. You found Uncle and the others." Tears glisten on his cheeks. Mr. Williams comes over, his face drawn with weariness.

"You and Finder saved those men," he says. "You were right. The dog knew where to look. As head of the Illinois Mine Experiment and Mine Life Saving Station, I can tell you that we are always looking for new methods of mine safety and recovery. I believe there is a job on our team for you and your dog."

Thomas's eyes widen. "You mean to rescue people underground?"

Mr. Williams nods. "There are many accidents like this. Rarely as traumatic as the fire here in Cherry. But workers often get lost or suffer an injury on the job, and the team could use help to find them. What do *you* think, young man? You and your dog would be an asset."

Thomas stoops. "Finder? What do you think? We'd still be going underground. But no more digging, shoveling, or pulling carts."

I woof, not sure of the question, but I hear the excitement in Thomas's voice. I dance around his legs despite my sore paws, wagging my tail, showing him that I am excited too.

Thomas laughs, then shakes Mr. William's hand. "Thank you, sir. We would be honored."

As Mr. Williams heads back to the tower, the people on the other side of the barricade begin to point. "That's Finder. He's the coal mine dog who helped rescue the others," someone calls. "He's a hero!"

"*Hero! Hero!*"

Confused by the shouts, Thomas and I look around. A reporter pushes past a guard. "Is it true, son? Is your dog a hero?" He holds up a big camera and a flash of light explodes. I press against Thomas's legs, shrinking from the man and the noise.

"No. It is not true," Thomas answers. "He did find the survivors, but he was only doing his job." There is pride in his voice, and I nuzzle his bandaged hand. "The men who died in the fire trying to save others—like Mr. Norberg, Mr. Dovin, Mr. Bundy, and Ole Freiburg—they are the real heroes."

Brushing past the reporter, Thomas hurries back toward the air shaft. "I hope I spoke for you, Finder," he says to me. "After all, you *are* a hero. But more importantly, you did your job and saved the trapped miners."

He smiles down at me. "I know you're tired and it is late. But our work is not done tonight. If there are more men below, we need to find them."

Giving him a toothy smile, I dance beside him even though we are heading back to the air shaft. The moon is bright and I can see branches reaching for the sky. I can hear the whisper of critters in the brush. I can smell the fresh, rain-spattered earth.

But I must go below again with Thomas because I have a new job now. I will not be searching for coal in the black, twisty tunnels. I will be searching for survivors.

And when I come back to the surface, I will strut proudly. Not because I am a hero, but because I am a mine rescue dog.

The History Behind *Finder*

The Cherry Mine Disaster

The St. Paul Coal Mine located in Cherry, Illinois, also known as the Cherry Mine, was considered one of the safest and most modern in the United States. It was also the scene of one of the worst disasters. On November 13, 1909, a fire started in a coal car that was used to transport hay for the mules. Instead of warning the miners, workers and officials tried to put it out. Despite their efforts, the flames quickly grew larger. Most of the miners did not know about the fire until the end of the day. When they came to the shaft to be hoisted to the surface, the flames had spread to the cage and it was burning too. For most, it was too late to escape.

Miraculously, twenty of the men who were trapped underground survived for eight days.

In August 1910, a state mine inspector reported 256 men dead or lost in the Cherry Mine fire. This included twelve of the rescuers and several victims who were listed as seventeen years old.

Finder and Thomas are fictional characters. But George Eddy, Alex Norberg, Walter Waite, and other men in the story—many who died in the disaster while trying to save others—were real.

Coal Mining and Miners

During the Civil War, the coal mining industry boomed as rail transport expanded and the need for fuel increased. Mine companies used a process called "room and pillar" mining. Men would dig a "room," hauling out the coal. They'd leave behind a floor-to-ceiling "pillar" of rock, earth, and stones large enough to support the tunnel roof. Timbers were used for support as needed.

To loosen the coal from the rock, miners drilled holes in the rich seams, which were then filled with explosives. Once the coal and rock had been blasted into smaller chunks, an assistant called a "butty" or "buddy" like Thomas would shovel it into the cars. He worked until he'd filled five to six cars, reaching "full coal." It was grueling and dangerous work.

Blasting the seams released poisonous gases into the air. All miners feared "black damp," a mix of nitrogen and carbon dioxide that killed miners who were exposed to it. Sometimes, blasting also caused cave-ins. "I got caught under a big rock, and I couldn't get out. My leg was broken. There I was all alone. No light. Complete darkness," one buddy said after a roof collapsed (Bartoletti, *Growing Up in Coal Country,* page 61). Other miners like Mr. McKinny died of black lung, a disease caused by inhaling coal dust.

Miners ran the risk of being burned, drowned, suffocated, or crushed. Even today, mining is a dangerous job. On April 5, 2010, almost one hundred years after the Cherry Mine disaster, twenty-nine miners were killed at the Upper Big Branch Mine in West Virginia.

Young Mine Workers

Boys as young as seven were often employed in the mines. In 1900 the state of Illinois outlawed the hiring of children under the age of fourteen to work for wages. However, hard times drove many parents to lie about their sons' ages. A father would obtain a work certificate and fill in the required age. No proof was needed. Mine employers looked the other way since wages for children were cheaper than for adults, and children could work a variety of jobs.

A year before Finder's story begins, the National Child Labor Committee hired Lewis Hine as an "investigative reporter." Hine traveled across the country photographing children at work, many in the mines. In 1908, NCLC reported that "one out of every four mine workers was a boy, age seven to sixteen" (Bartoletti, *Growing Up in Coal Country,* page 120).

Many child workers were "breaker boys" in the coal mines. They sorted slate and rock from the coal. In the early 1900s, their pay was about 70 cents a day. From dawn until dusk the breaker boys sat hunched on wood benches as the coal rumbled past. They weren't allowed to wear gloves because they could pick out the coal better with bare hands. The work caused their fingers to swell and the skin to crack. Though they covered their mouths with rags, their lungs filled with soot and smoke. And they were almost always in danger of accidents.

Lewis Hine reported that "two breaker boys fell or were carried into the coal chute, where they were smothered to death" (Freedman, *Kids at Work: Lewis Hine and the Crusade Against Child Labor,* page 48).

Other boys, "trappers" like Seth in the story, opened and shut the large doors between tunnels. Workers called "spraggers" jabbed wooden poles (sprags) into the car wheels to control the speed. Other young workers drove mules or oiled machinery. All the jobs were hard, dirty, and dangerous. Still, it wasn't until 1938 that strict federal laws were enacted to protect child workers.

Animals in the Mines

Animals were used extensively in the mines. As early as 1911, British miners carried canaries into the tunnels to detect poisonous gases. If the canary stopped singing or died, the worker knew the tunnel was not safe. Canaries were finally phased out in 1987 when miners began using electronic gas detectors.

In 1900, more than 84 percent of coal was hauled by mules and horses. Ponies, goats, and dogs sometimes pulled smaller coal cars through narrow tunnels. In McDonough County, Illinois, thirty-one dogs similar to Finder were used to pull "empty and loaded cars of coal to and from the mines, to the bottom of the shaft or to the mouth of the drifts" (Twenty-Second Annual Coal Report).

Rats did not work in the mine, but they thrived in the dark tunnels. They ate mule feed, stole lunch pails, and begged for crusts. "You had to keep your lunch close by," said one miner. "They'd take any-thing—even your clothes if you left them lying around. They'd drag them away and hide them" (Bartoletti, *Growing Up in Coal Country,* page 50).

The Cur Dog

Finder is considered a mountain cur, which was not a recognized breed until 1957. The United Kennel Club did not list the cur as a breed until 1998.

Curs are often thought of as the original pioneer dog. It is believed that a type of cur came to America with Hernando de Soto in the 1500s. They bred with native dogs to become fast, sturdy, fierce hunters.

Later, the pioneers relied on their cur dogs for herding, guarding, and supplying food. After World War II, when people migrated to cities, the breed became scarce. Today, the mountain cur is one of about fourteen cur varieties, all considered working dogs.

A Real Mine Rescue Dog

In the early 1900s, there were no mine rescue dogs. But today, Ginny, a Dutch shepherd, works as a mine dog in Bristol, Virginia. Ginny uses her superior sense of smell to scent toxic gas from a mile away. She also wears a special beeper that warns of poisonous gases. As a member of the Alpha Rescue team, she is trained to find humans trapped in the Alpha Coal Mine as well as above ground.

Bibliography

Bartoletti, Susan Campbell. *Growing up in Coal Country*. Boston: Houghton Mifflin Co., 1996.

"Childhood Lost." Eastern Illinois University. *www.eiu.edu/eiutps/childhood.php.*

Crowell, D.L. *History of the Local Coal Mining Industry in Ohio: Ohio Division of Geological Survey Bulletin* 72: 1995.

Freedman, Russell. *Kids at Work: Lewis Hine and the Crusade Against Child Labor.* New York: Clarion Books, 1994.

History, Genealogy, Coal Mining in Illinois. Twenty-Second Annual Coal Report, 1903, Illinois Bureau of Labor Statistics, Springfield, ILL; Phillips Bros. State Printers, 1904.

Long, Susan Hill. *Whistle in the Dark*. New York: Holiday House, 2013.

Martin, Holly. "Ginny the Rescue Dog Saves Trapped and Injured Coal Miners." *Examiner.com.* June 1, 2002. *www.examiner.com.article/ginny-the-rescue-dog-saves-trapped-and-injured-coal-miners.*

Sherard, Gerald E. *Pennsylvania Mine Accidents.* Nov. 2011. *www.genealogy.com.*

Tintori, Karen. *Trapped: The 1909 Cherry Mine Disaster.* New York: Atria Books, 2002.

White, Thomas and Louis Murphy. "Eight Days in a Burning Mine." *The World Magazine.* Oct. 1911. *www.msha.gov.*

Websites

Information on Dogs
www.greatdogsite.com

Original Mountain Cur Breeders Association
www.omcba.homestead.com

United Kennel Club
www.ukcdogs.com

Ginny the Alpha Rescue Dog
www.alphaminerescuedog.com

Children and the Law
www.encyclopedia.chicagohistory.org/pages/279.html

Coal Mining Photos
http://hinton-gen.com/coal/photos.html

Information and Photos on Cherry Mine
guitarjourney.tripod.com/cherrycoalminedisaster

About the Author

When Alison Hart was seven years old, she wrote, illustrated, and self-published a book called *The Wild Dog*. Since then, she's authored more than twenty books for young readers, including the *Dog Chronicles* series, *Anna's Blizzard, Emma's River*, and the *Racing to Freedom* trilogy. She lives in Virginia.

www.alisonhartbooks.com

About the Illustrator

Michael G. Montgomery creates illustrations for advertising, magazines and posters, and children's books, including the *Dog Chronicles* series, *First Dog Fala*, and *Night Rabbits*. He lives in Georgia with his family and two dogs.

www.michaelgmontgomery.com

Also in the series

Darling, Mercy Dog of World War I

Written by Alison Hart
Illustrated by Michael G. Montgomery
HC: 978-1-56145-705-2

When the British military asks families to volunteer their dogs to help the war effort, Darling is sent off to be trained as a mercy dog. She helps locate injured soldiers on the battlefield, despite gunfire, poisonous gases, and other dangers. She is skilled at her job, but surrounded by danger. Will she ever make it back home to England?

"Wartime adventure with plenty of heart."

—*Kirkus Reviews*

Murphy, Gold Rush Dog

Written by Alison Hart
Illustrated by Michael G. Montgomery
HC: 978-1-56145-769-4

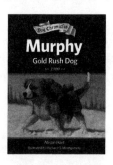

Sally and her mother have just arrived in Nome, Alaska, intent
on joining the other gold seekers and making a new life there.
Yet even with Murphy at their side, life in the mining town is
harsh and forbidding. When it seems they may have to give up
and return to Seattle, Sally and Murphy decide to strike out on
their own, hoping to find gold and make a permanent home.

"Equal parts heart-wrenching and -warming...
An adventure-filled tale set within a fascinating
period of history."

—*Kirkus Reviews*

Also by Alison Hart

Anna's Blizzard
HC: 978-1-56145-349-8

Anna loves life on the Nebraska prairie where she lives with her parents and four-year-old brother in a simple sod house. She doesn't mind helping out with chores on her family's farm, especially when she is herding sheep with her pony. When a fierce blizzard suddenly kicks up on a mild winter day, Anna, her schoolmates, and their teacher become trapped in the one-room schoolhouse. The kerosene is gone and the wood for the stove is low. Then the wind tears away the roof and door. Anna knows they must escape before it is too late. Does she have the courage and strength to lead the others through the whiteout to safety?

"Anna is a strong, appealing heroine, and the story is suspenseful..."
—School Library Journal

Emma's River
HC: 978-1-56145-524-9

Emma and her mama have boarded the *Sally May* for a steamboat journey that will take them to St. Joseph, where Papa will be waiting. When concern over her pony lures Emma below to the main deck—a place that she has been forbidden to go—she is shocked by what she encounters. Here is a world completely different from the pampered one above with its comfortable stateroom and fine food. Livestock and poor immigrants huddle together—underfed, unclean, and exhausted. Soon Emma is making regular trips below, ferrying food to Patrick, a young stowaway who recently emigrated from Ireland. When the boiler explodes and the steamboat starts sinking, Emma fights her way through the black smoke to find her friends and family. But is it too late?

"There's never a dull moment..." —BOOKLIST

THE RACING TO FREEDOM TRILOGY
Gabriel's Horses
HC: 978-1-56145-398-6
PB: 978-1-56145-528-7

Gabriel is the son of a free black father and a slave mother, which makes him a slave as well. He loves to help his father care for the thoroughbred racehorses on Master Giles's farm and hopes to become a famous jockey one day. But the violence of war disrupts the familiar routine of daily life on the farm. When Gabriel's father enlists in a Colored Battalion to help the Union Army and earn enough money to purchase freedom for his wife and son, Gabriel is both proud and worried. But the absence of his father brings the arrival of a white horse trainer with harsh, cruel methods for handling horses...and people. Now it is up to Gabriel to protect the horses he loves.

"At the core of this stirring historical novel is the question of what freedom means... The boy's first-person, present-tense narrative brings close the thrilling horse racing—on the plantation, at the race course, and in the war—and the African American history in all its complexity."
—BOOKLIST

Gabriel's Triumph
HC: 978-1-56145-410-5
PB: 978-1-56145-547-8

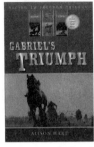

Recently freed, Gabriel is making a name for himself as a jockey. When his former master asks him to ride a powerful but unpredictable horse, in a prestigious race, Gabriel jumps at the chance to compete against some of the greatest jockeys in the business. But as soon as he begins the journey to Saratoga, he finds that high-stakes horse racing can be a nasty business—and that being freed is not the same as being free.

Gabriel's Journey
HC: 978-1-56145-442-6
PB: 978-1-56145-530-0

Gabriel leaves behind his successful horse racing career to join his parents at Camp Nelson, where his father is a sergeant in the Fifth U.S. Colored Calvary of the Union Army. When the Calvary receives orders to join white regiments in an attack on the Virginia salt works, Gabriel surreptitiously gets ahold of a horse and a uniform and joins the troops. But being a soldier is a lot harder than he imagined. Bad, weather, rough riding, dwindling supplies, and blatant racism wear heavily on his spirit. When his father doesn't return from battle, Gabriel must go in search of him.